ROBERT LOUIS STEVENSON

KIDNAPPED

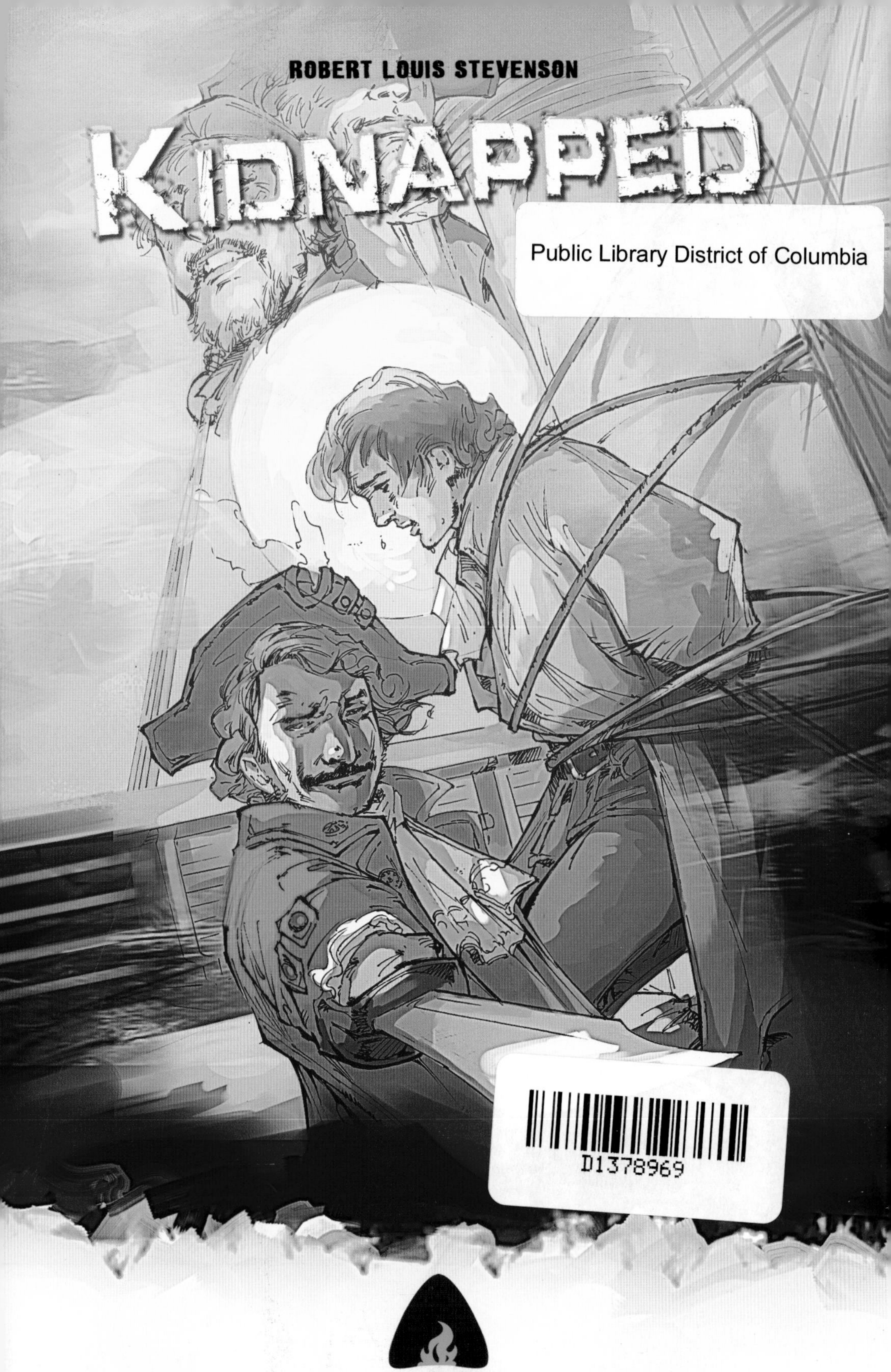

CAMPFIRE™

KALYANI NAVYUG MEDIA PVT. LTD
New Delhi

ROBERT LOUIS STEVENSON

KIDNAPPED

Sitting around the Campfire, telling the story, were:

AUTHOR ROBERT LOUIS STEVENSON
WORDSMITH MARK JONES
ILLUSTRATOR NARESH KUMAR
COLORIST MANOJ YADAV & VINOD S. PILLAI
LETTERER BHAVNATH CHAUDHARY
EDITORS DIVYA DUBEY & EMAN CHOWDHARY
EDITOR (INFORMATIVE CONTENT) PUSHPANJALI BOROOAH
ART DIRECTOR RAJESH NAGULAKONDA
PRODUCTION CONTROLLER VISHAL SHARMA
COVER ART NARESH KUMAR & ANIL C. K.
DESIGNER JAYAKRISHNAN K. P.

CAMPFIRE™ GRAPHIC NOVELS
www.campfire.co.in

Published by Kalyani Navyug Media Pvt. Ltd. 101 C, Shiv House, Hari Nagar Ashram
New Delhi 110014 India
ISBN: 978-93-80028-52-1

Printed in India at Rave India

ABOUT THE AUTHOR

Robert Louis Stevenson was born in Edinburgh, Scotland, in 1850. The son of an engineer, Stevenson followed in his father's footsteps by studying engineering and law at the University of Edinburgh. However, his passion for writing soon became more than a hobby, and he decided to pursue it on a full-time basis. This career choice initially upset his father, but Stevenson made a promise to complete his studies, and was admitted to the Scottish Bar in 1875.

Stevenson's most famous work is the classic pirate tale *Treasure Island*, that was published in 1883. A fast-paced story of adventure, it soon became popular across the world. In the 125 years since then, readers of all ages have delighted in following the exploits of young Jim Hawkins as he travels to a remote island in search of buried gold. Stevenson later created an infamous, but very intriguing, character in *The Strange Case of Dr. Jekyll and Mr. Hyde*, published in 1886. His adventure story *Kidnapped*, a tale of a young boy and a stolen inheritance, was also published in the same year.

Throughout his life, Stevenson was frequently in poor health, and he often traveled abroad in search of places with mild climates. He also wrote a number of essays detailing these trips. During one such journey to France, he met an American woman named Frances Osbourne, and later married her during a visit to California.

In 1887, Stevenson headed for America with his wife, stepson, and mother. He had become famous in New York, and received many attractive offers from various publishers. It was soon after this move that he began writing *The Master of Ballantrae*, a novel that is considered one of his best works.

Stevenson eventually settled with his family on the island of Samoa, where he died at the age of forty-four on December 3, 1894. While best known for writing tales of action and adventure, Robert Louis Stevenson is also remembered as an accomplished poet and essayist.

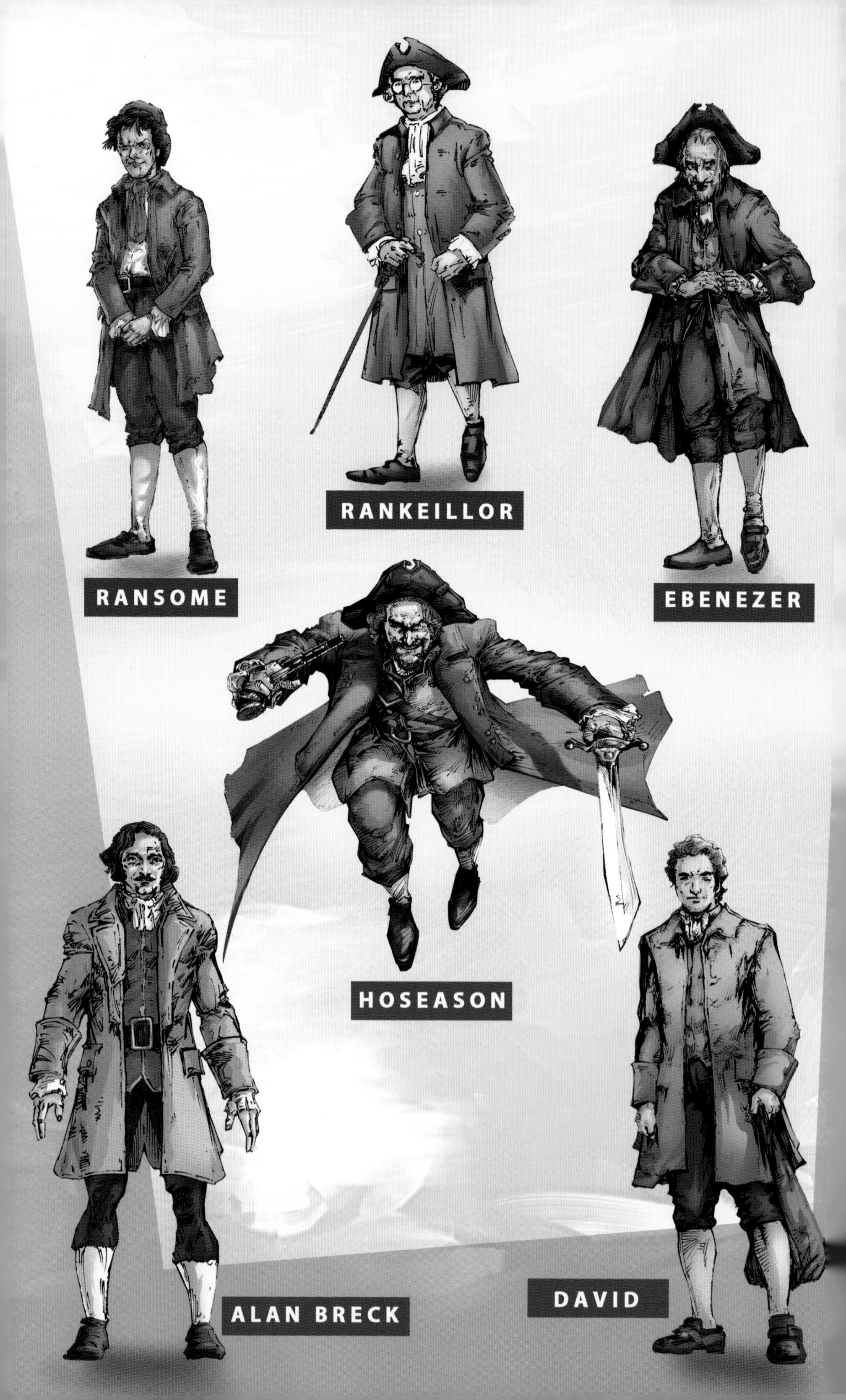
RANKEILLOR
RANSOME
EBENEZER
HOSEASON
ALAN BRECK
DAVID

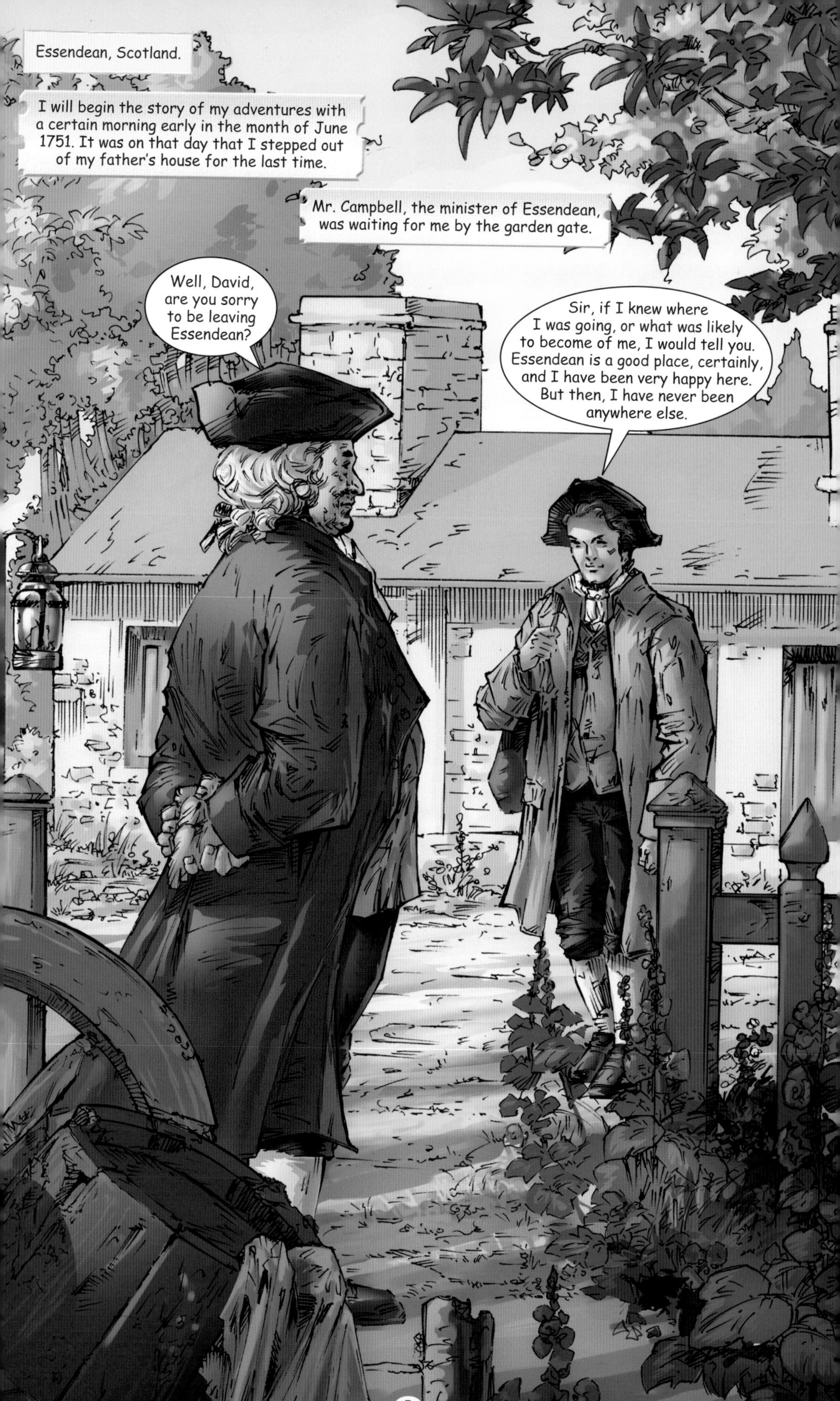

Essendean, Scotland.
I will begin the story of my adventures with a certain morning early in the month of June 1751. It was on that day that I stepped out of my father's house for the last time.
Mr. Campbell, the minister of Essendean, was waiting for me by the garden gate.
Well, David, are you sorry to be leaving Essendean?
Sir, if I knew where I was going, or what was likely to become of me, I would tell you. Essendean is a good place, certainly, and I have been very happy here. But then, I have never been anywhere else.

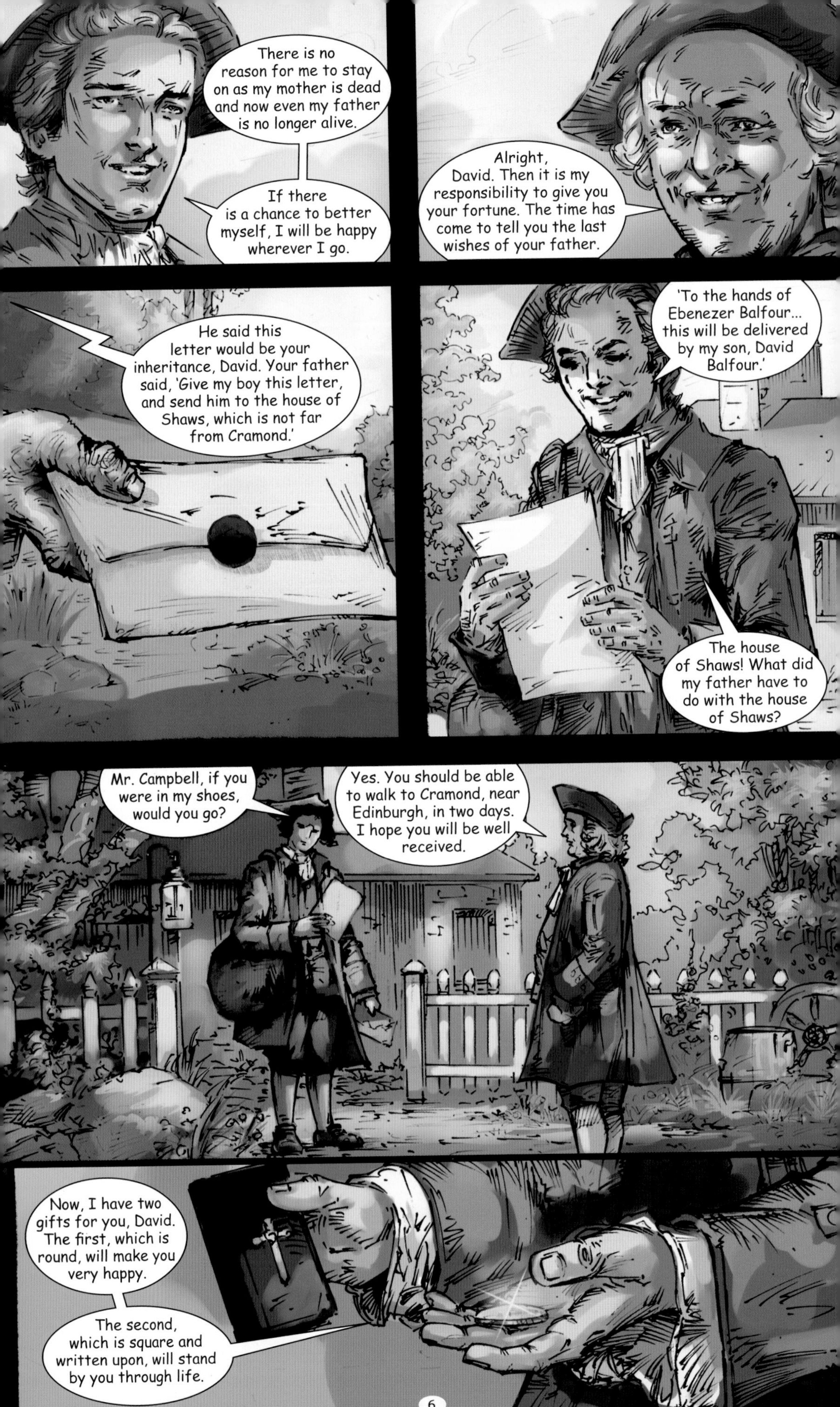
There is no reason for me to stay on as my mother is dead and now even my father is no longer alive.
If there is a chance to better myself, I will be happy wherever I go.
Alright, David. Then it is my responsibility to give you your fortune. The time has come to tell you the last wishes of your father.
He said this letter would be your inheritance, David. Your father said, 'Give my boy this letter, and send him to the house of Shaws, which is not far from Cramond.'
'To the hands of Ebenezer Balfour... this will be delivered by my son, David Balfour.'
The house of Shaws! What did my father have to do with the house of Shaws?
Mr. Campbell, if you were in my shoes, would you go?
Yes. You should be able to walk to Cramond, near Edinburgh, in two days. I hope you will be well received.
Now, I have two gifts for you, David. The first, which is round, will make you very happy.
The second, which is square and written upon, will stand by you through life.

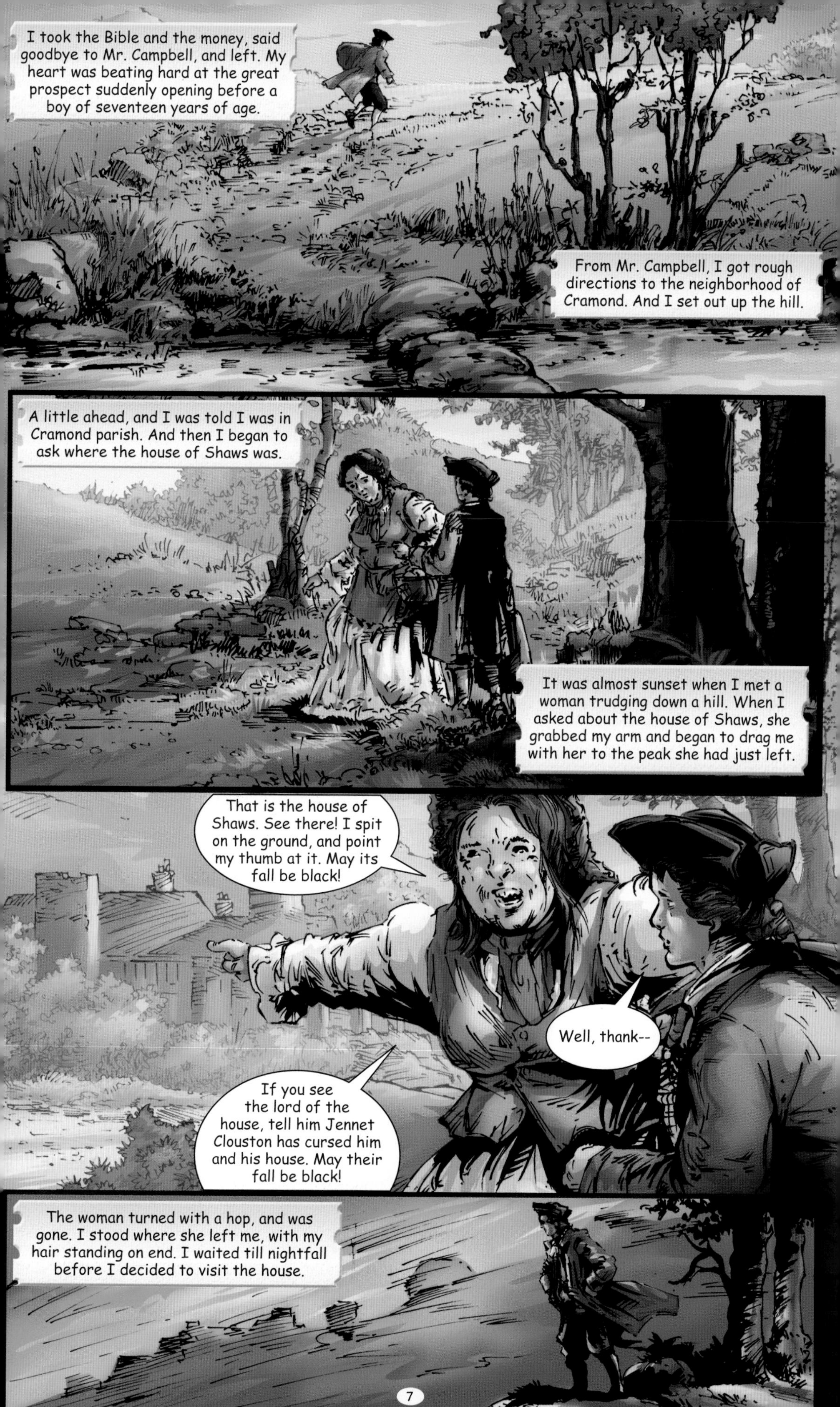
I took the Bible and the money, said goodbye to Mr. Campbell, and left. My heart was beating hard at the great prospect suddenly opening before a boy of seventeen years of age.
From Mr. Campbell, I got rough directions to the neighborhood of Cramond. And I set out up the hill.
A little ahead, and I was told I was in Cramond parish. And then I began to ask where the house of Shaws was.
It was almost sunset when I met a woman trudging down a hill. When I asked about the house of Shaws, she grabbed my arm and began to drag me with her to the peak she had just left.
That is the house of Shaws. See there! I spit on the ground, and point my thumb at it. May its fall be black!
Well, thank--
If you see the lord of the house, tell him Jennet Clouston has cursed him and his house. May their fall be black!
The woman turned with a hop, and was gone. I stood where she left me, with my hair standing on end. I waited till nightfall before I decided to visit the house.

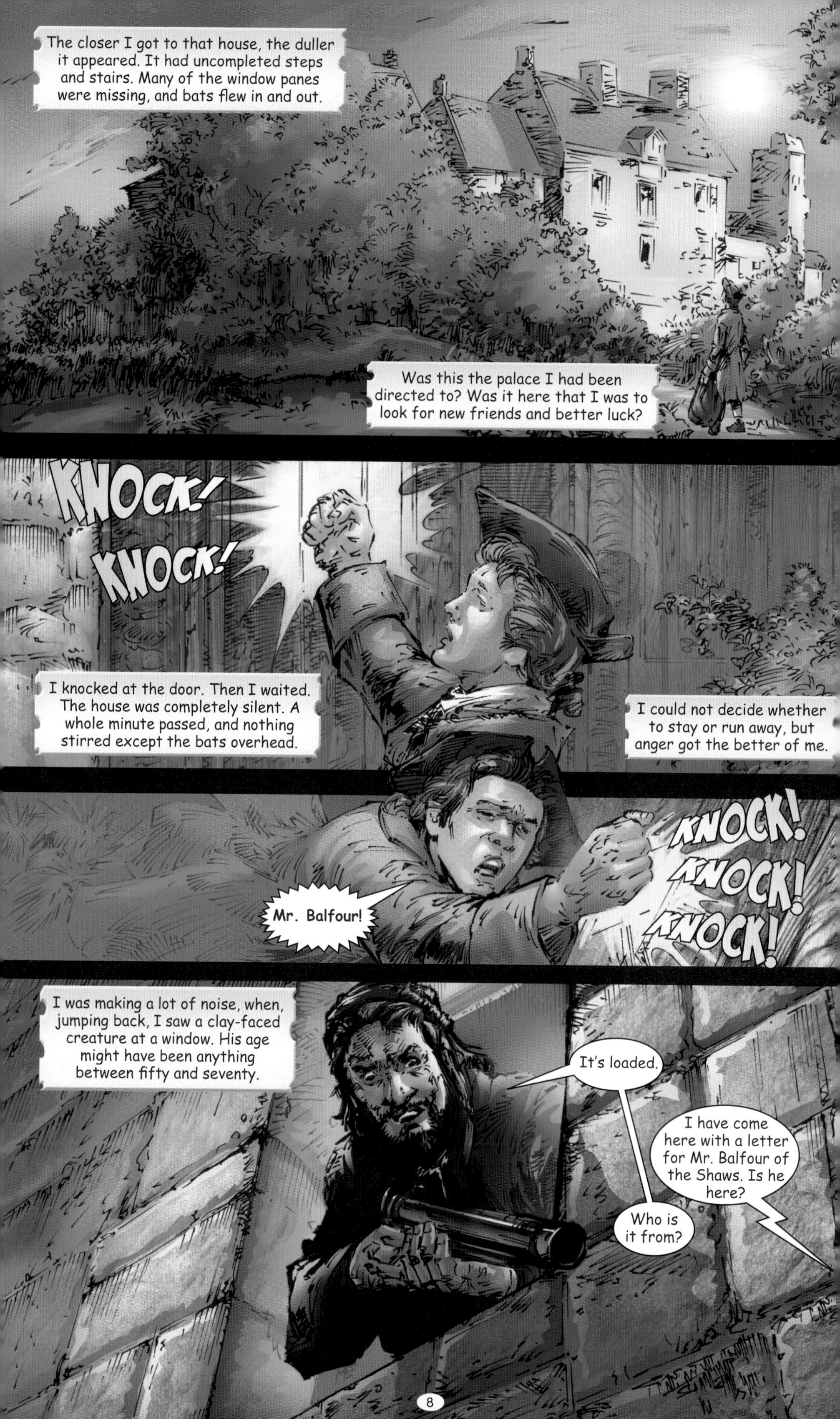
The closer I got to that house, the duller it appeared. It had uncompleted steps and stairs. Many of the window panes were missing, and bats flew in and out.
Was this the palace I had been directed to? Was it here that I was to look for new friends and better luck?
KNOCK!
KNOCK!
I knocked at the door. Then I waited. The house was completely silent. A whole minute passed, and nothing stirred except the bats overhead.
I could not decide whether to stay or run away, but anger got the better of me.
Mr. Balfour!
KNOCK!
KNOCK!
KNOCK!
I was making a lot of noise, when, jumping back, I saw a clay-faced creature at a window. His age might have been anything between fifty and seventy.
It's loaded.
I have come here with a letter for Mr. Balfour of the Shaws. Is he here?
Who is it from?

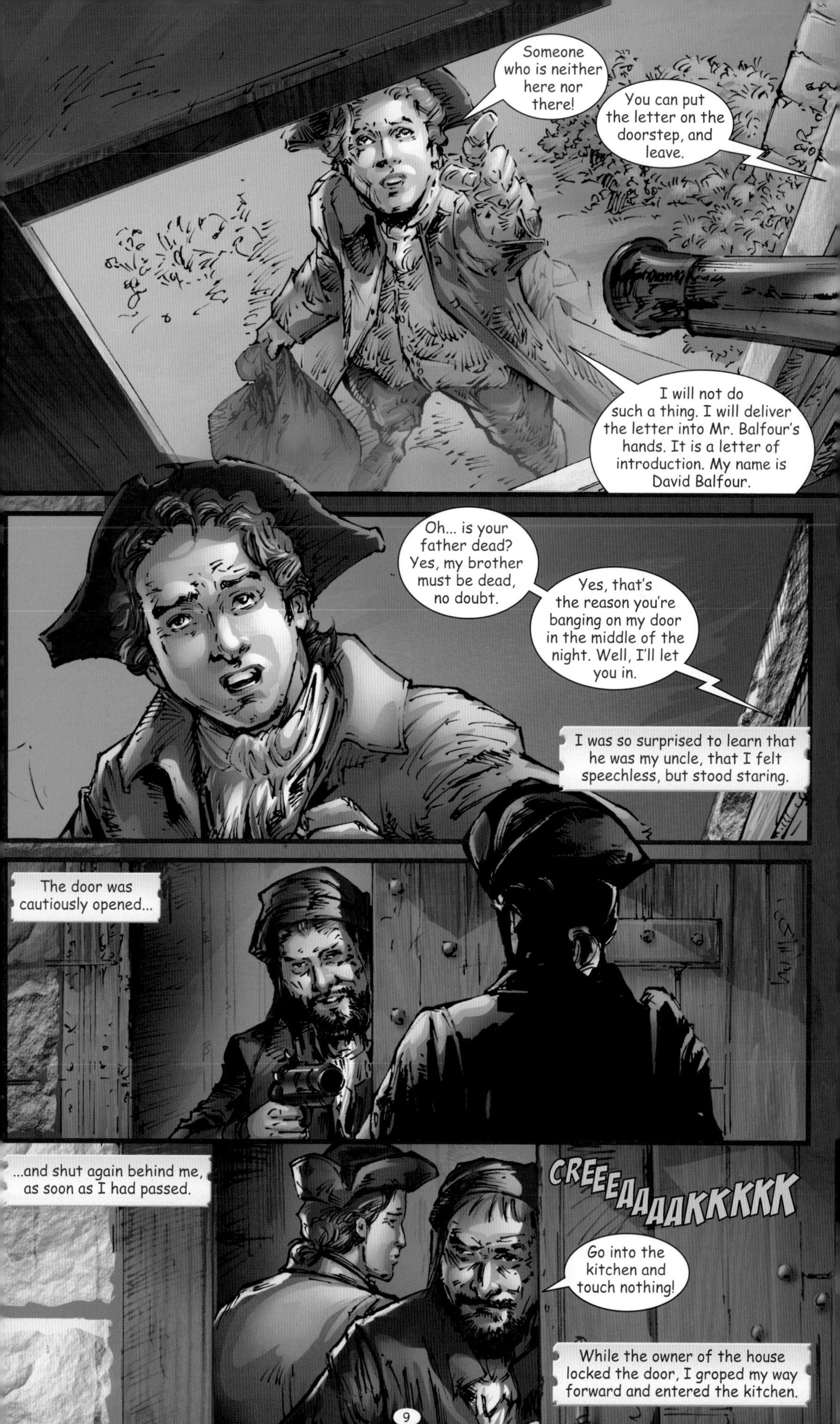

Someone who is neither here nor there!
You can put the letter on the doorstep, and leave.
I will not do such a thing. I will deliver the letter into Mr. Balfour's hands. It is a letter of introduction. My name is David Balfour.
Oh... is your father dead? Yes, my brother must be dead, no doubt.
Yes, that's the reason you're banging on my door in the middle of the night. Well, I'll let you in.
I was so surprised to learn that he was my uncle, that I felt speechless, but stood staring.
The door was cautiously opened...
...and shut again behind me, as soon as I had passed.
CREEEAAAAKKKKK
Go into the kitchen and touch nothing!
While the owner of the house locked the door, I groped my way forward and entered the kitchen.

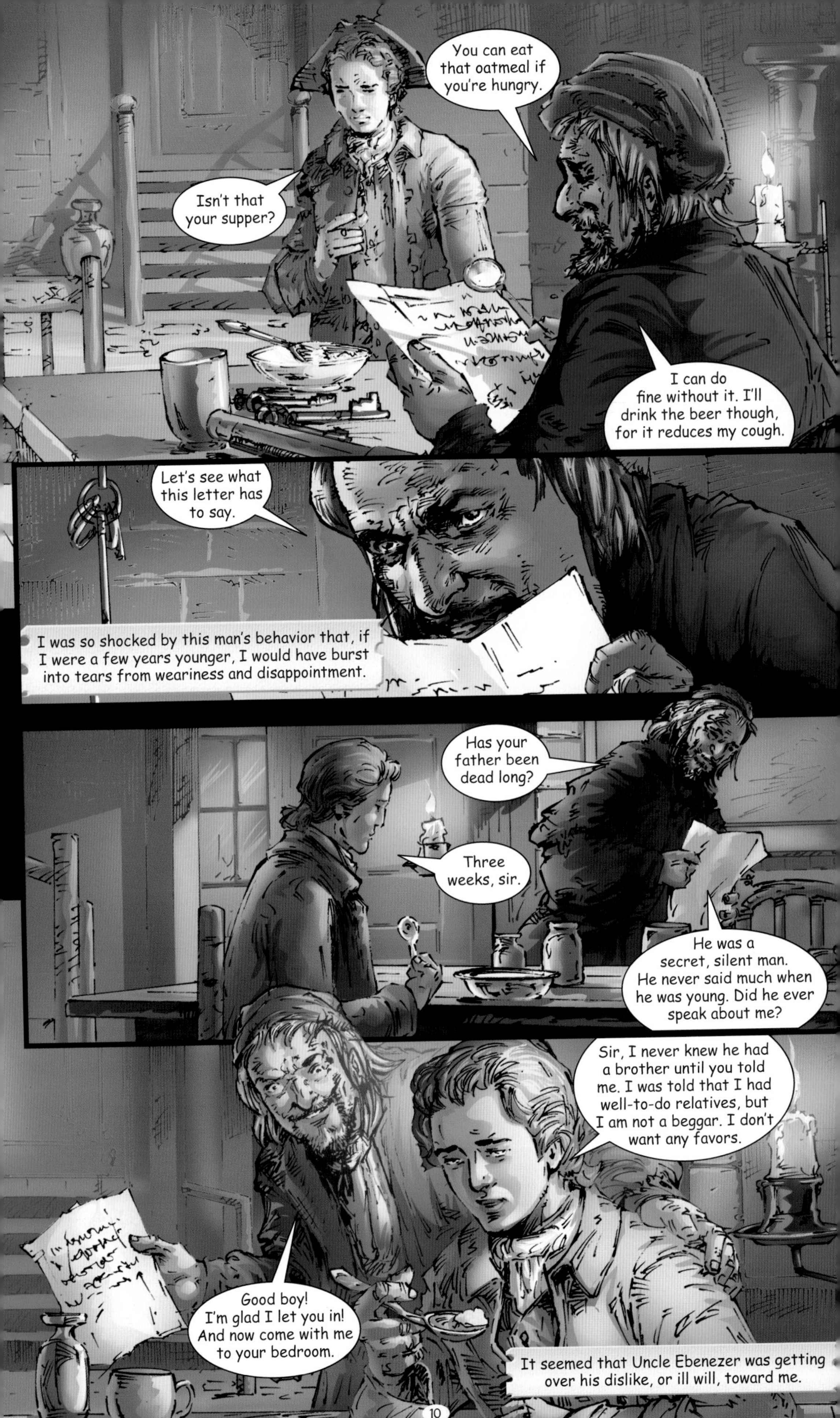

You can eat that oatmeal if you're hungry.
Isn't that your supper?
I can do fine without it. I'll drink the beer though, for it reduces my cough.
Let's see what this letter has to say.
I was so shocked by this man's behavior that, if I were a few years younger, I would have burst into tears from weariness and disappointment.
Has your father been dead long?
Three weeks, sir.
He was a secret, silent man. He never said much when he was young. Did he ever speak about me?
Sir, I never knew he had a brother until you told me. I was told that I had well-to-do relatives, but I am not a beggar. I don't want any favors.
Good boy! I'm glad I let you in! And now come with me to your bedroom.
It seemed that Uncle Ebenezer was getting over his dislike, or ill will, toward me.

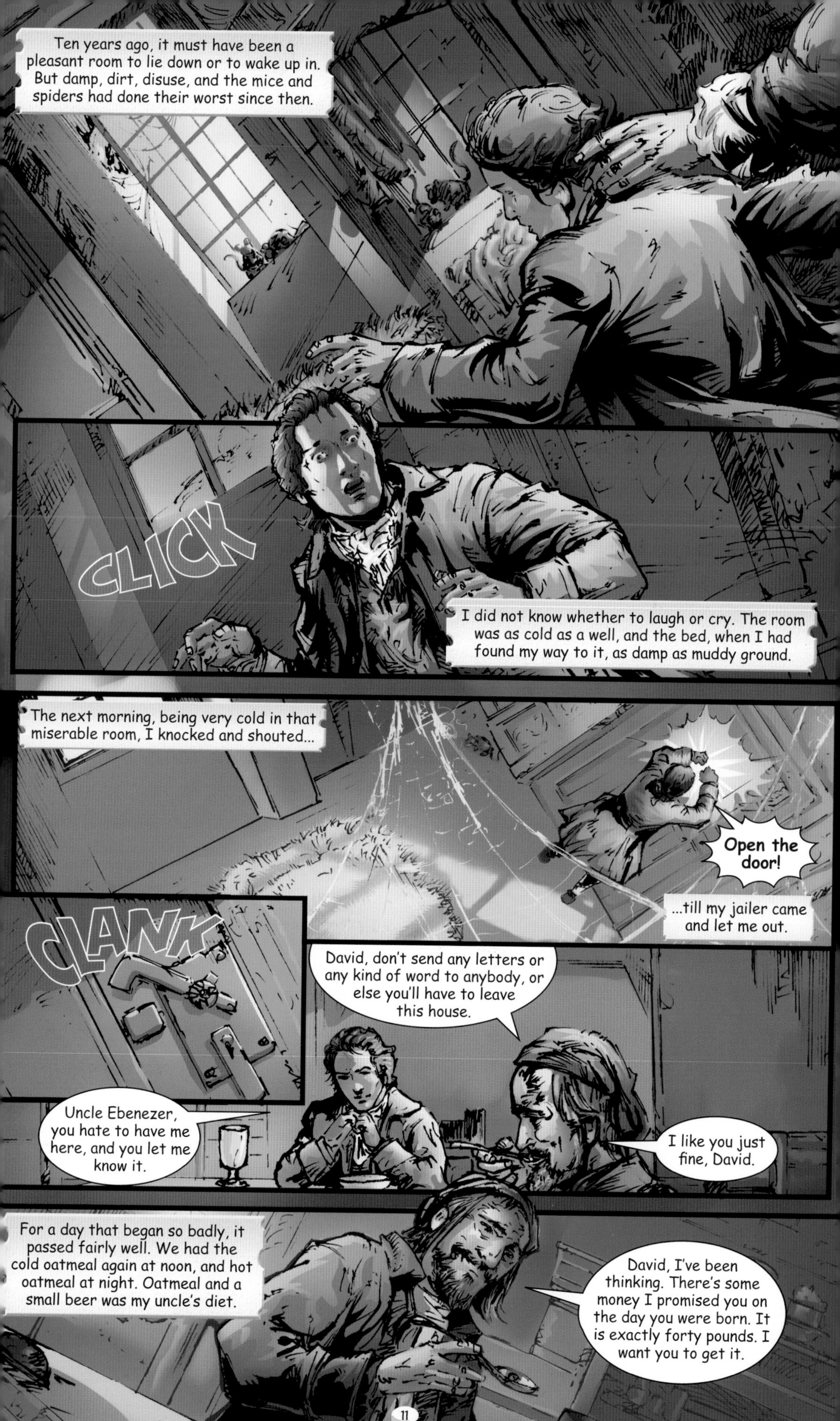
Ten years ago, it must have been a pleasant room to lie down or to wake up in. But damp, dirt, disuse, and the mice and spiders had done their worst since then.
CLICK
I did not know whether to laugh or cry. The room was as cold as a well, and the bed, when I had found my way to it, as damp as muddy ground.
The next morning, being very cold in that miserable room, I knocked and shouted...
Open the door!
...till my jailer came and let me out.
CLANK
David, don't send any letters or any kind of word to anybody, or else you'll have to leave this house.
Uncle Ebenezer, you hate to have me here, and you let me know it.
I like you just fine, David.
For a day that began so badly, it passed fairly well. We had the cold oatmeal again at noon, and hot oatmeal at night. Oatmeal and a small beer was my uncle's diet.
David, I've been thinking. There's some money I promised you on the day you were born. It is exactly forty pounds. I want you to get it.

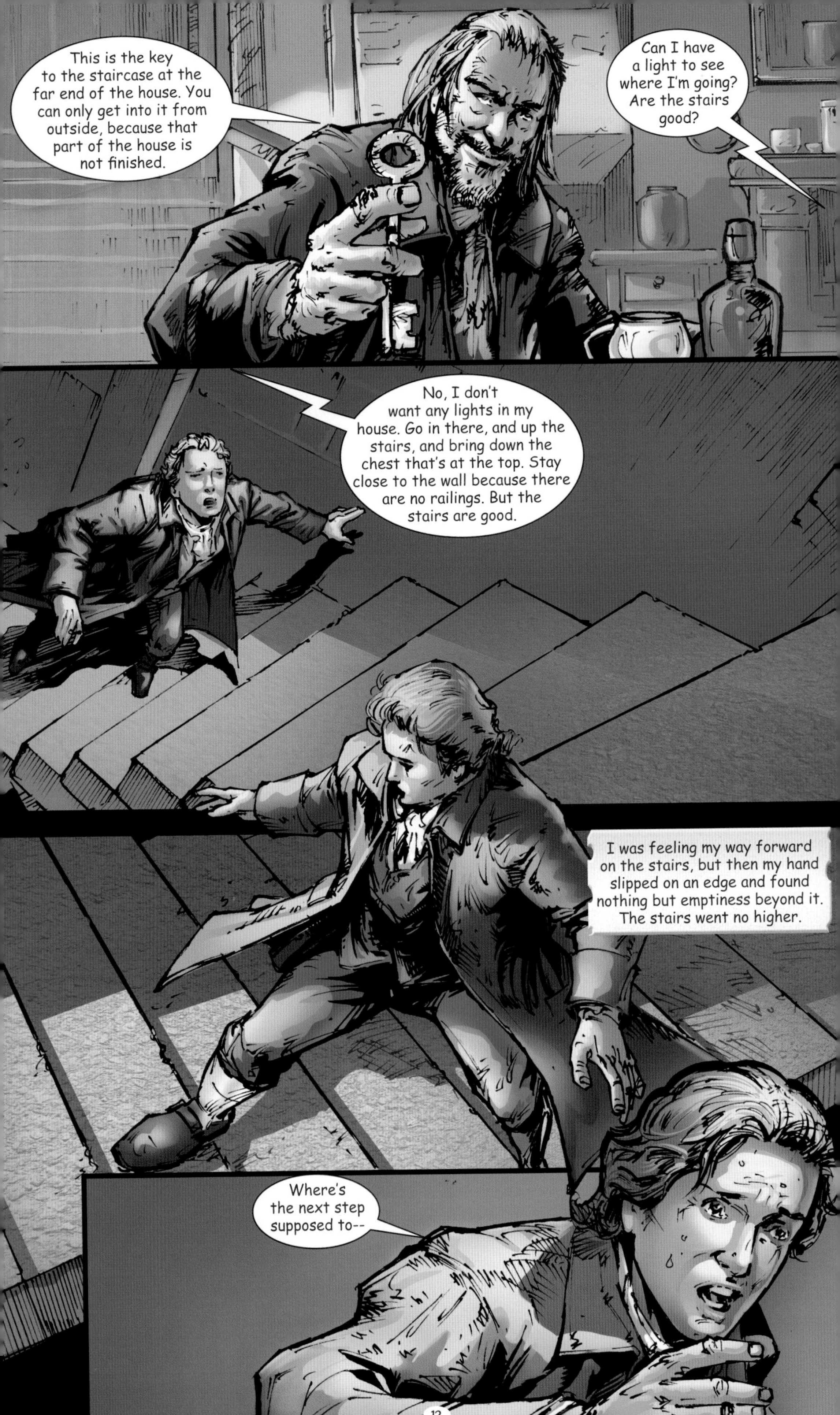
This is the key to the staircase at the far end of the house. You can only get into it from outside, because that part of the house is not finished.
Can I have a light to see where I'm going? Are the stairs good?
No, I don't want any lights in my house. Go in there, and up the stairs, and bring down the chest that's at the top. Stay close to the wall because there are no railings. But the stairs are good.
I was feeling my way forward on the stairs, but then my hand slipped on an edge and found nothing but emptiness beyond it. The stairs went no higher.
Where's the next step supposed to--

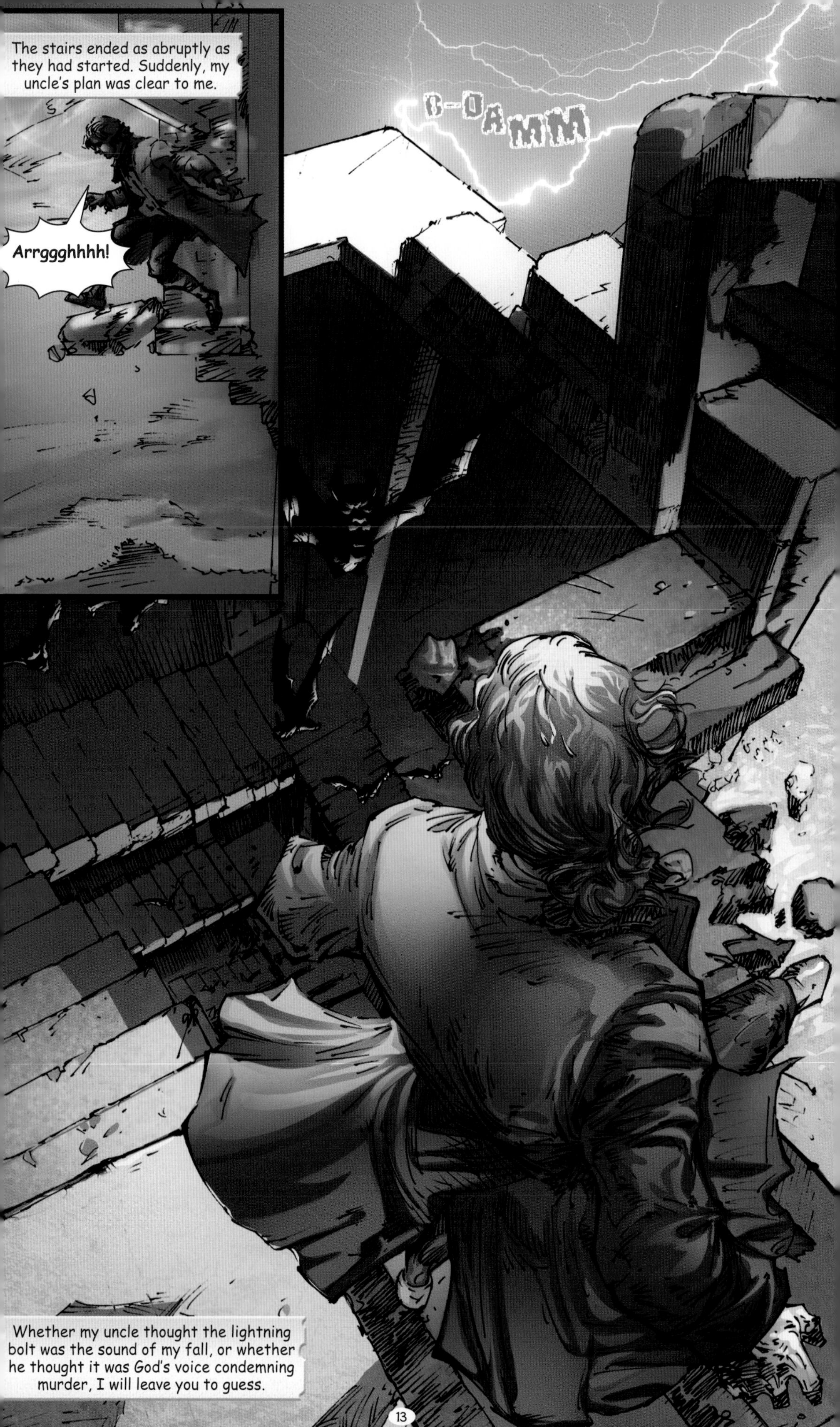

The stairs ended as abruptly as they had started. Suddenly, my uncle's plan was clear to me.
Arrggghhhh!
B-OAMMM
Whether my uncle thought the lightning bolt was the sound of my fall, or whether he thought it was God's voice condemning murder, I will leave you to guess.

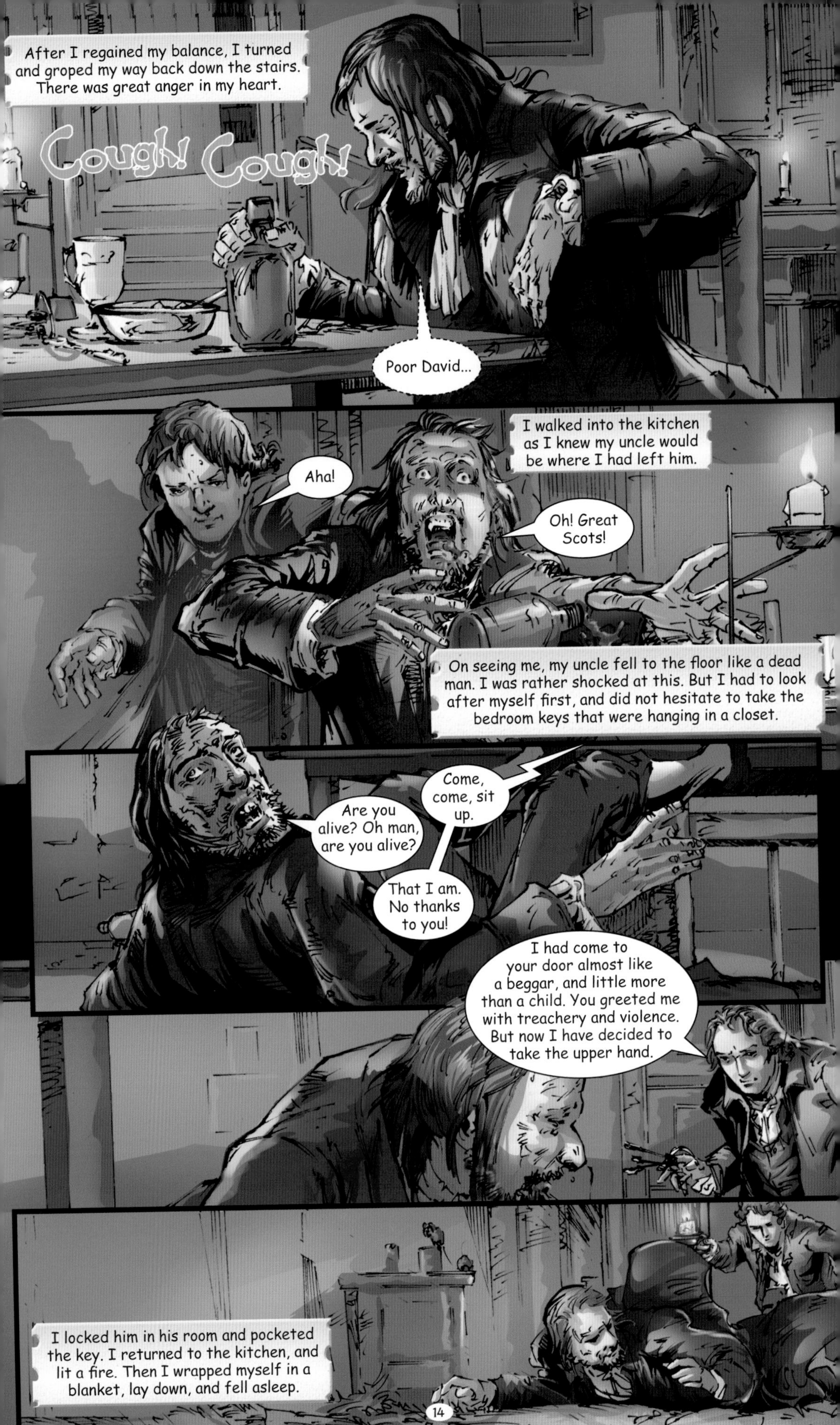
After I regained my balance, I turned and groped my way back down the stairs. There was great anger in my heart.
Cough! Cough!
Poor David...
I walked into the kitchen as I knew my uncle would be where I had left him.
Aha!
Oh! Great Scots!
On seeing me, my uncle fell to the floor like a dead man. I was rather shocked at this. But I had to look after myself first, and did not hesitate to take the bedroom keys that were hanging in a closet.
Are you alive? Oh man, are you alive?
Come, come, sit up.
That I am. No thanks to you!
I had come to your door almost like a beggar, and little more than a child. You greeted me with treachery and violence. But now I have decided to take the upper hand.
I locked him in his room and pocketed the key. I returned to the kitchen, and lit a fire. Then I wrapped myself in a blanket, lay down, and fell asleep.

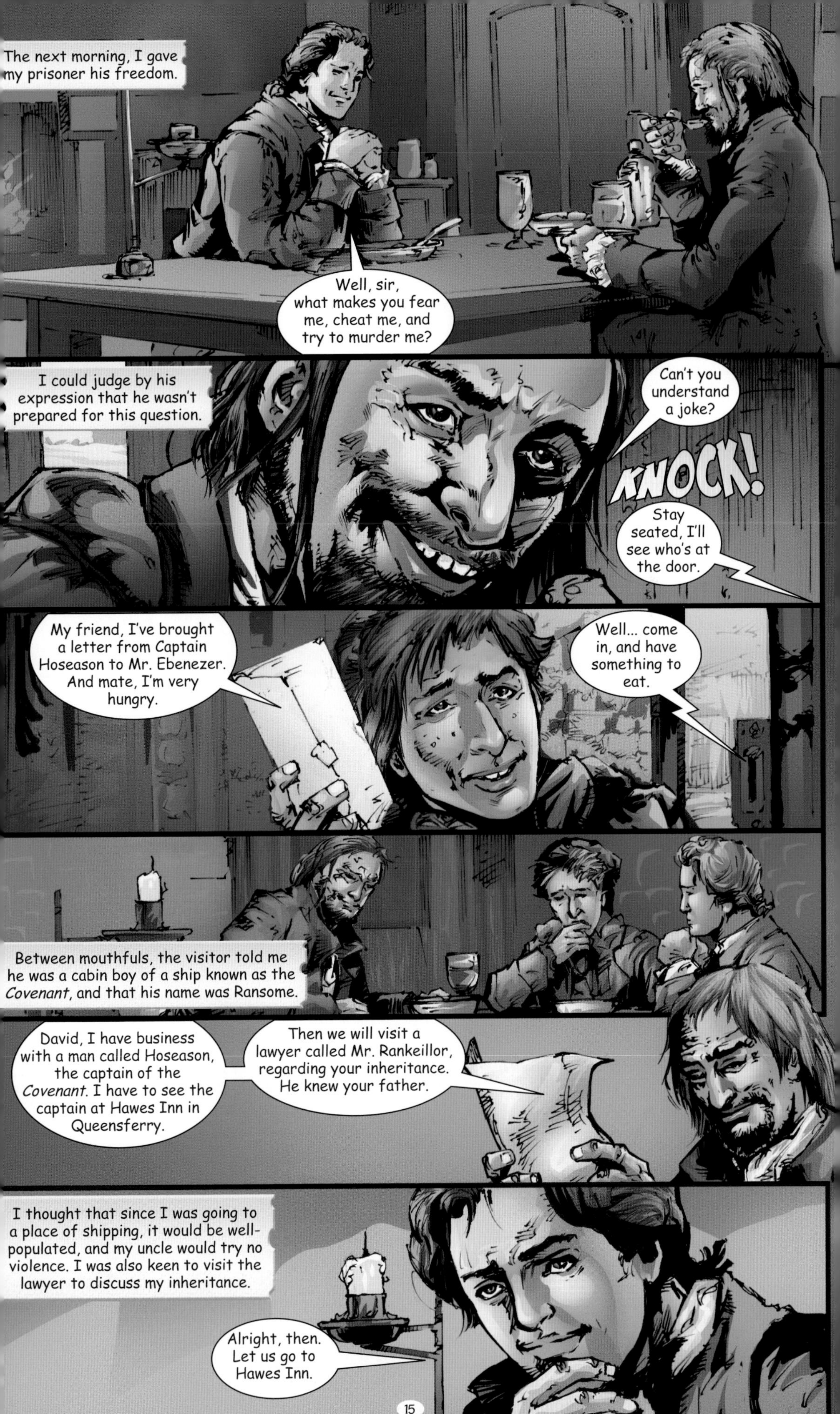

The next morning, I gave my prisoner his freedom.
Well, sir, what makes you fear me, cheat me, and try to murder me?
I could judge by his expression that he wasn't prepared for this question.
Can't you understand a joke?
KNOCK!
Stay seated, I'll see who's at the door.
My friend, I've brought a letter from Captain Hoseason to Mr. Ebenezer. And mate, I'm very hungry.
Well... come in, and have something to eat.
Between mouthfuls, the visitor told me he was a cabin boy of a ship known as the *Covenant*, and that his name was Ransome.
David, I have business with a man called Hoseason, the captain of the *Covenant*. I have to see the captain at Hawes Inn in Queensferry.
Then we will visit a lawyer called Mr. Rankeillor, regarding your inheritance. He knew your father.
I thought that since I was going to a place of shipping, it would be well-populated, and my uncle would try no violence. I was also keen to visit the lawyer to discuss my inheritance.
Alright, then. Let us go to Hawes Inn.

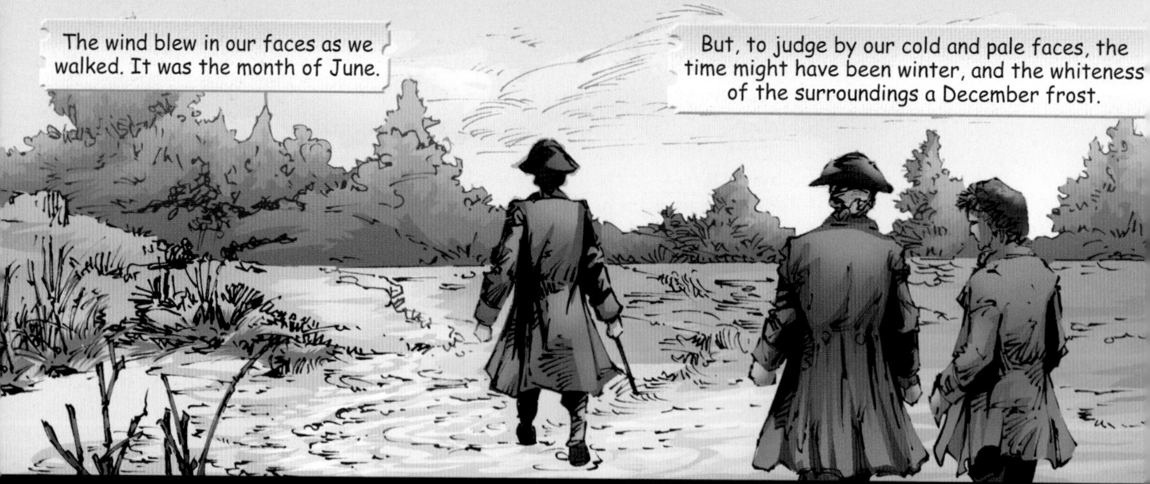
The wind blew in our faces as we walked. It was the month of June.
But, to judge by our cold and pale faces, the time might have been winter, and the whiteness of the surroundings a December frost.

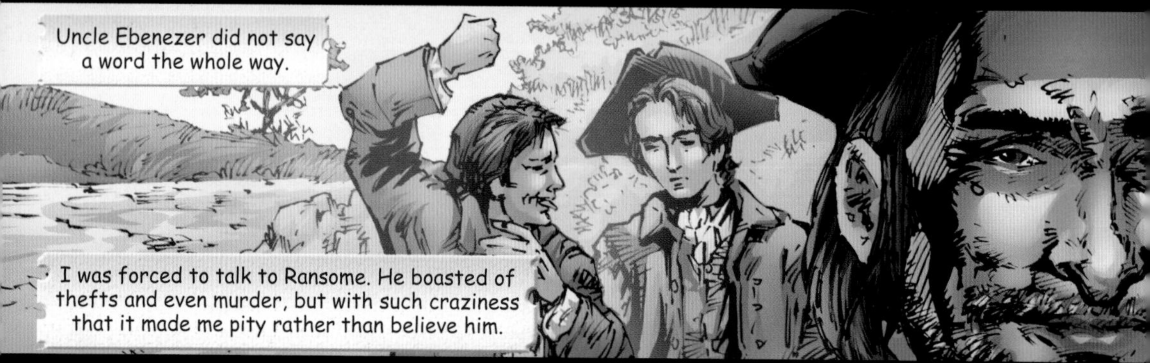
Uncle Ebenezer did not say a word the whole way.
I was forced to talk to Ransome. He boasted of thefts and even murder, but with such craziness that it made me pity rather than believe him.

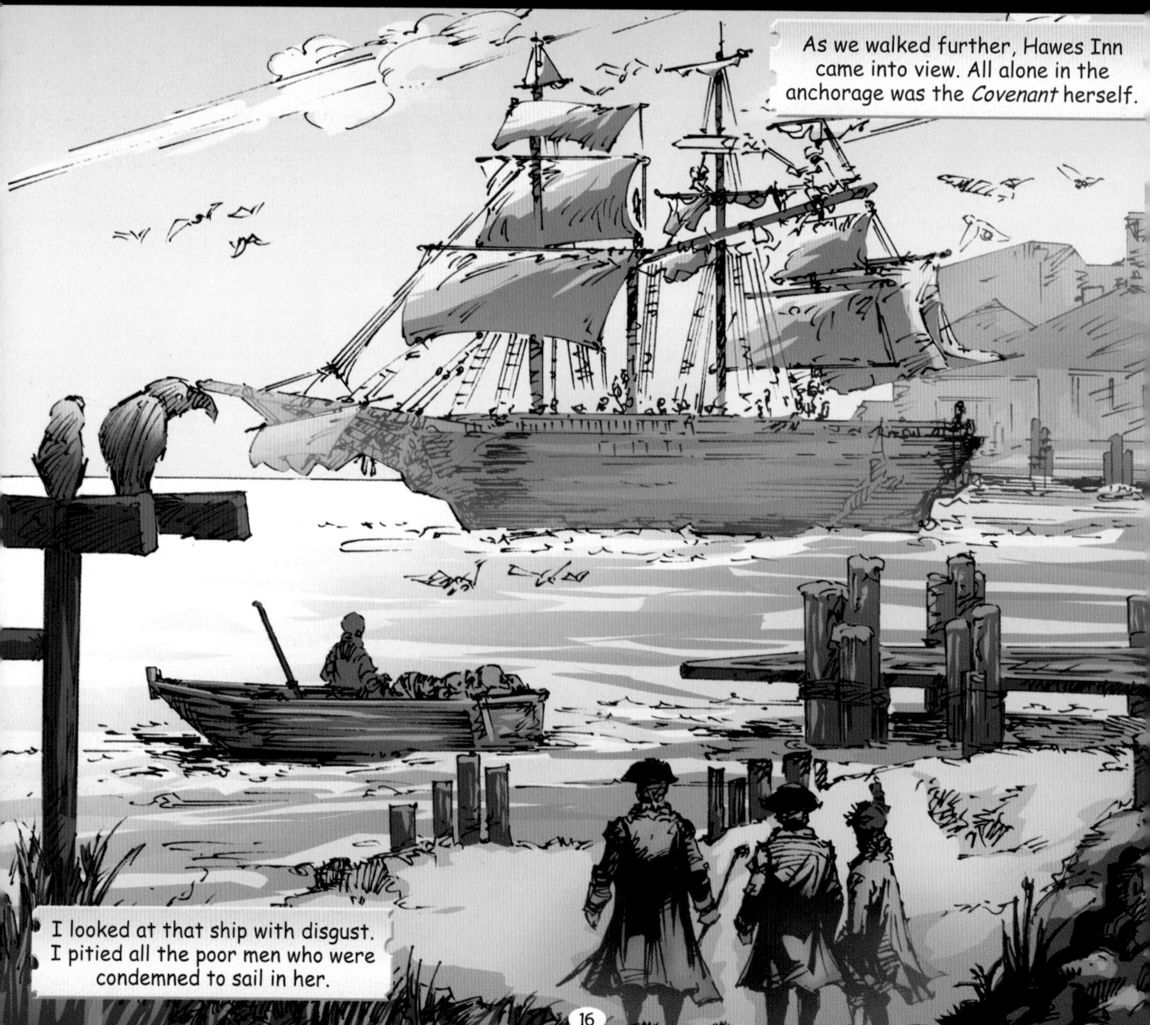
As we walked further, Hawes Inn came into view. All alone in the anchorage was the *Covenant* herself.
I looked at that ship with disgust. I pitied all the poor men who were condemned to sail in her.

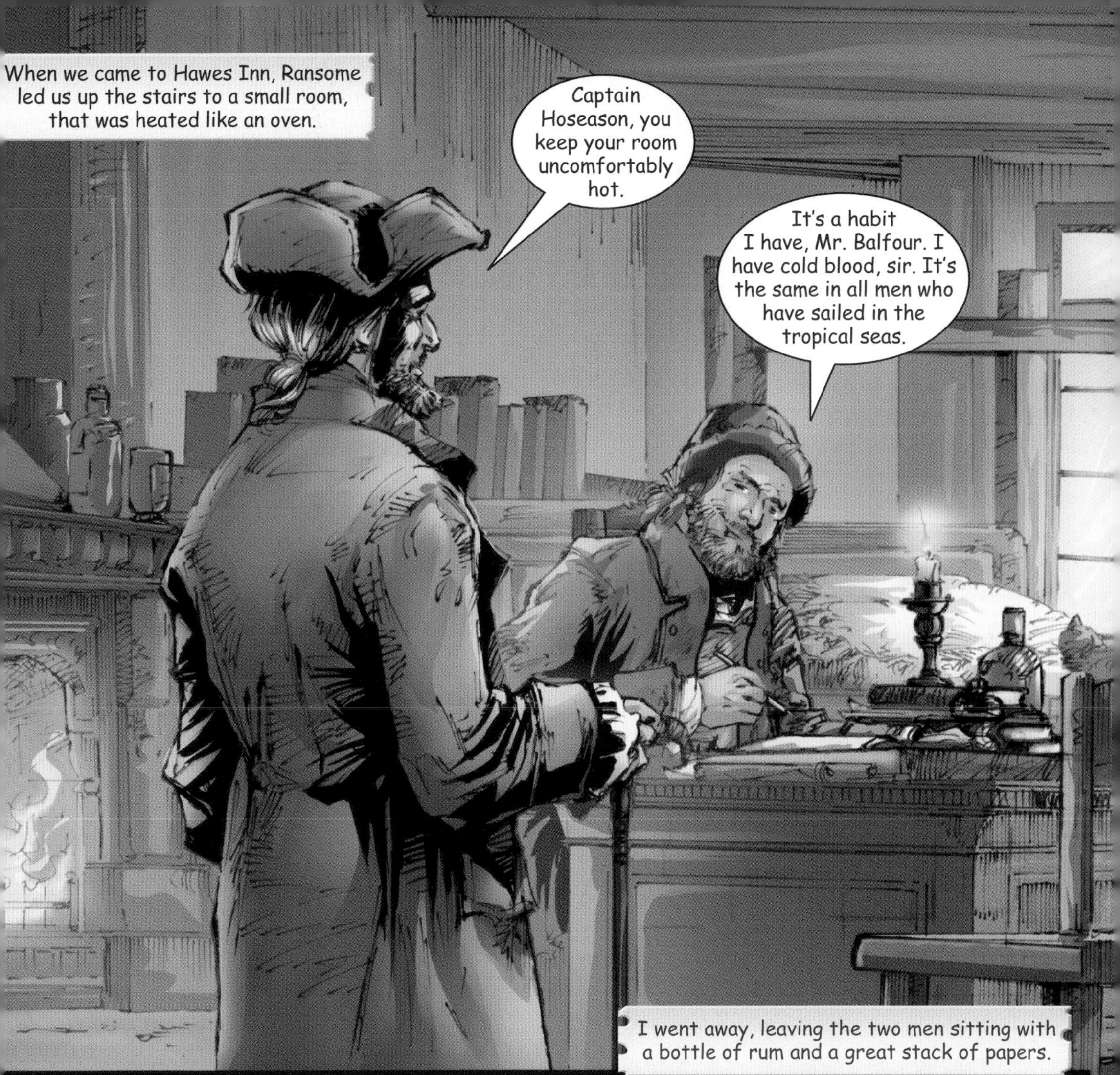
When we came to Hawes Inn, Ransome led us up the stairs to a small room, that was heated like an oven.
Captain Hoseason, you keep your room uncomfortably hot.
It's a habit I have, Mr. Balfour. I have cold blood, sir. It's the same in all men who have sailed in the tropical seas.
I went away, leaving the two men sitting with a bottle of rum and a great stack of papers.

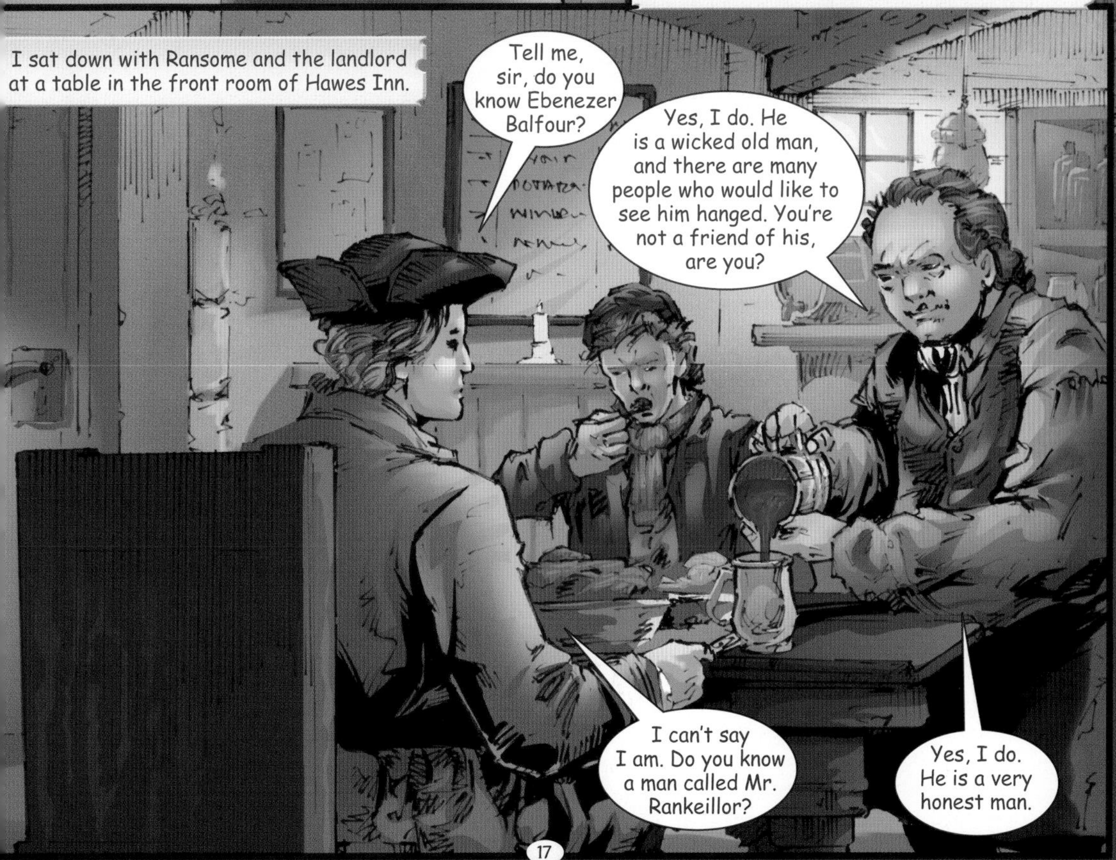
I sat down with Ransome and the landlord at a table in the front room of Hawes Inn.
Tell me, sir, do you know Ebenezer Balfour?
Yes, I do. He is a wicked old man, and there are many people who would like to see him hanged. You're not a friend of his, are you?
I can't say I am. Do you know a man called Mr. Rankeillor?
Yes, I do. He is a very honest man.

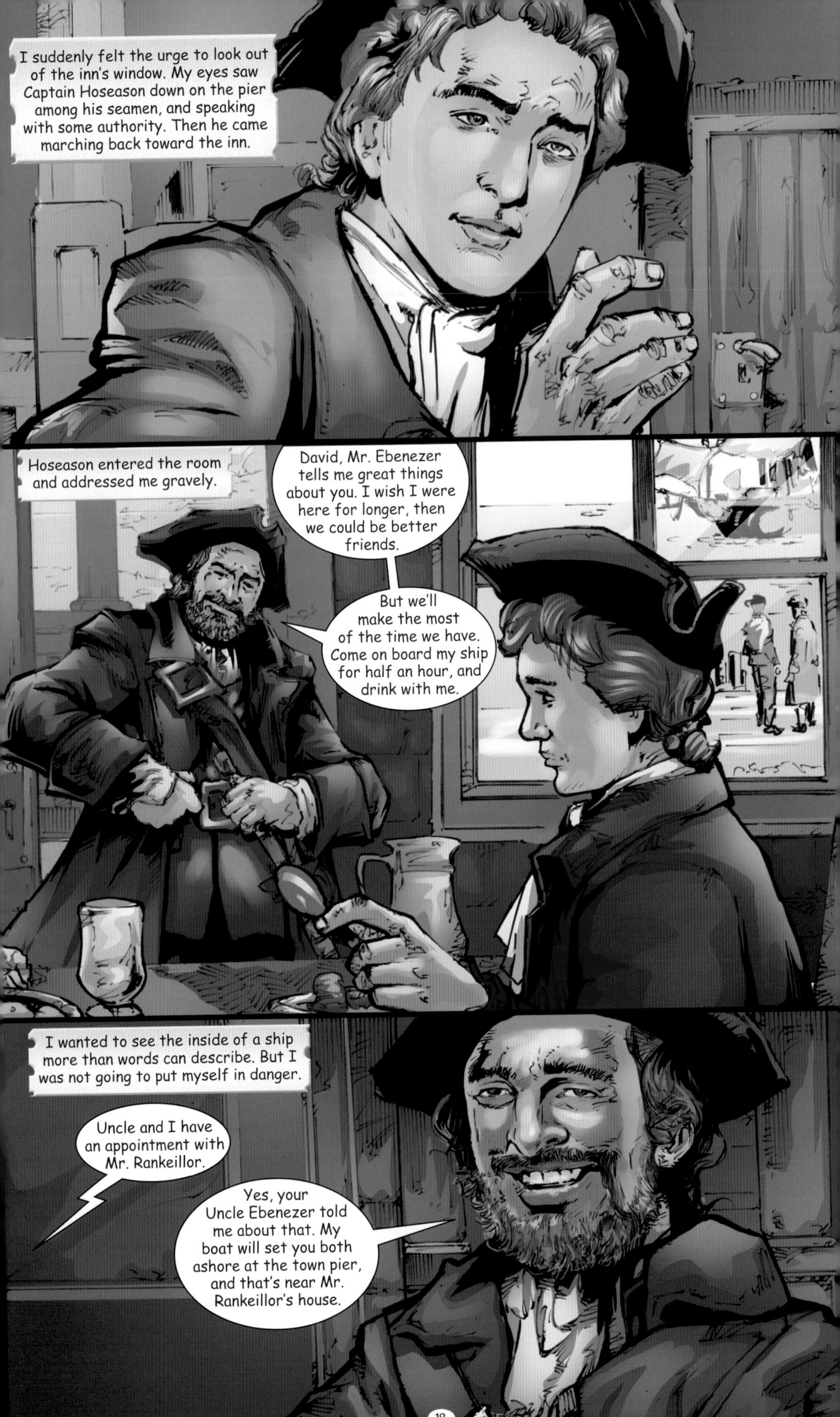
I suddenly felt the urge to look out of the inn's window. My eyes saw Captain Hoseason down on the pier among his seamen, and speaking with some authority. Then he came marching back toward the inn.
Hoseason entered the room and addressed me gravely.
David, Mr. Ebenezer tells me great things about you. I wish I were here for longer, then we could be better friends.
But we'll make the most of the time we have. Come on board my ship for half an hour, and drink with me.
I wanted to see the inside of a ship more than words can describe. But I was not going to put myself in danger.
Uncle and I have an appointment with Mr. Rankeillor.
Yes, your Uncle Ebenezer told me about that. My boat will set you both ashore at the town pier, and that's near Mr. Rankeillor's house.

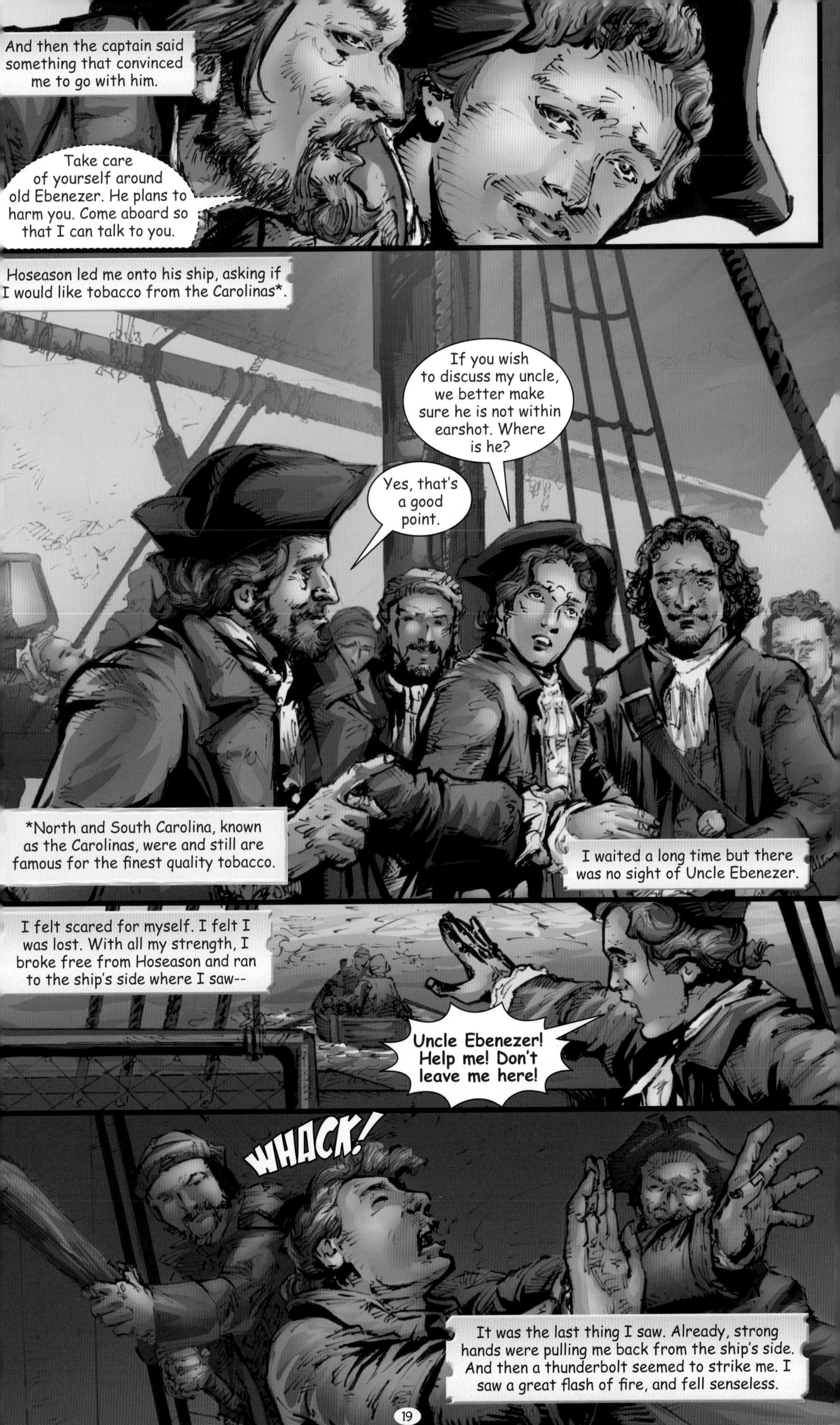

And then the captain said something that convinced me to go with him.
Take care of yourself around old Ebenezer. He plans to harm you. Come aboard so that I can talk to you.
Hoseason led me onto his ship, asking if I would like tobacco from the Carolinas*.
If you wish to discuss my uncle, we better make sure he is not within earshot. Where is he?
Yes, that's a good point.
*North and South Carolina, known as the Carolinas, were and still are famous for the finest quality tobacco.
I waited a long time but there was no sight of Uncle Ebenezer.
I felt scared for myself. I felt I was lost. With all my strength, I broke free from Hoseason and ran to the ship's side where I saw--
Uncle Ebenezer! Help me! Don't leave me here!
WHACK!
It was the last thing I saw. Already, strong hands were pulling me back from the ship's side. And then a thunderbolt seemed to strike me. I saw a great flash of fire, and fell senseless.

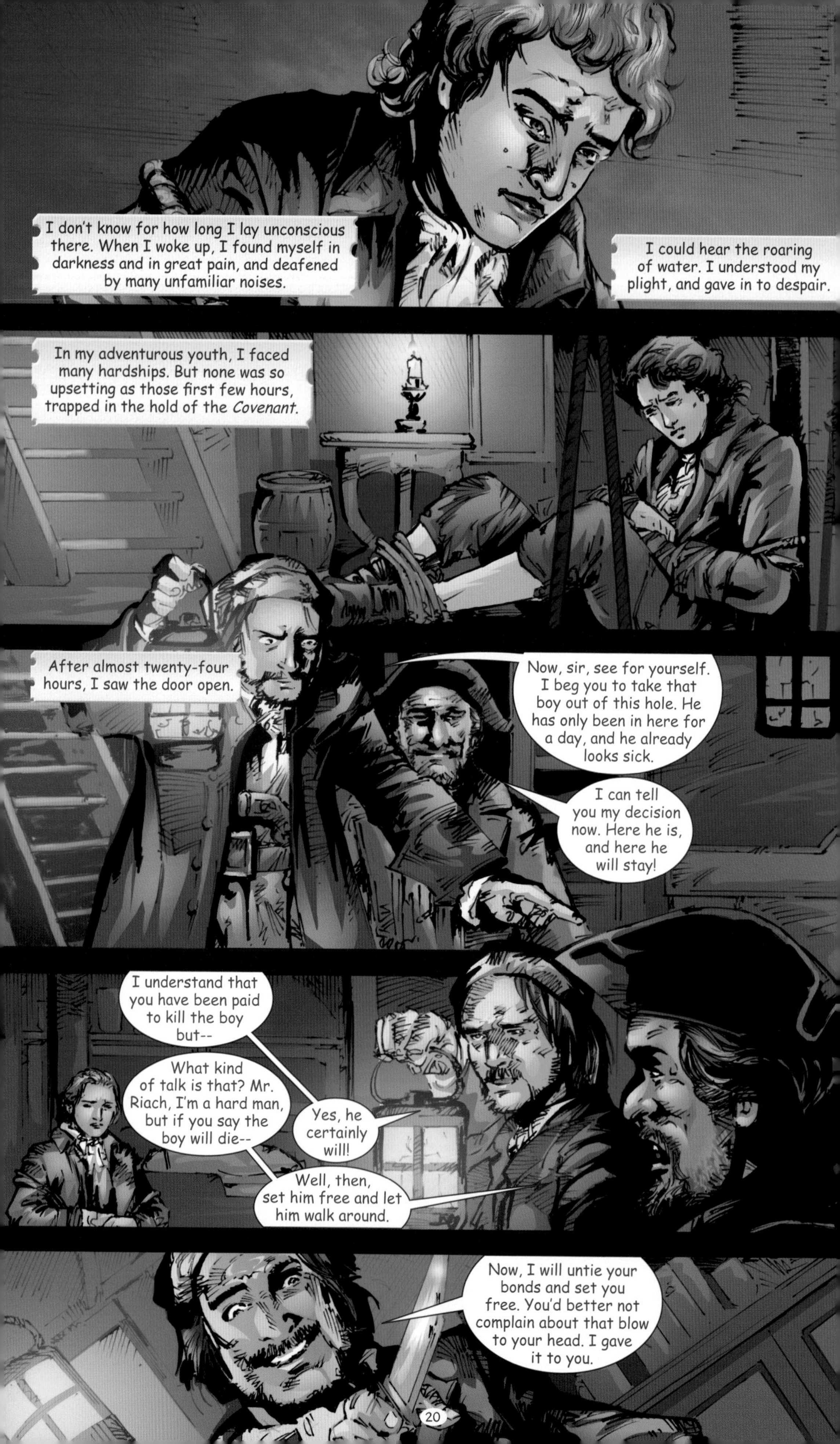
I don't know for how long I lay unconscious there. When I woke up, I found myself in darkness and in great pain, and deafened by many unfamiliar noises.
I could hear the roaring of water. I understood my plight, and gave in to despair.
In my adventurous youth, I faced many hardships. But none was so upsetting as those first few hours, trapped in the hold of the *Covenant*.
After almost twenty-four hours, I saw the door open.
Now, sir, see for yourself. I beg you to take that boy out of this hole. He has only been in here for a day, and he already looks sick.
I can tell you my decision now. Here he is, and here he will stay!
I understand that you have been paid to kill the boy but--
What kind of talk is that? Mr. Riach, I'm a hard man, but if you say the boy will die--
Yes, he certainly will!
Well, then, set him free and let him walk around.
Now, I will untie your bonds and set you free. You'd better not complain about that blow to your head. I gave it to you.

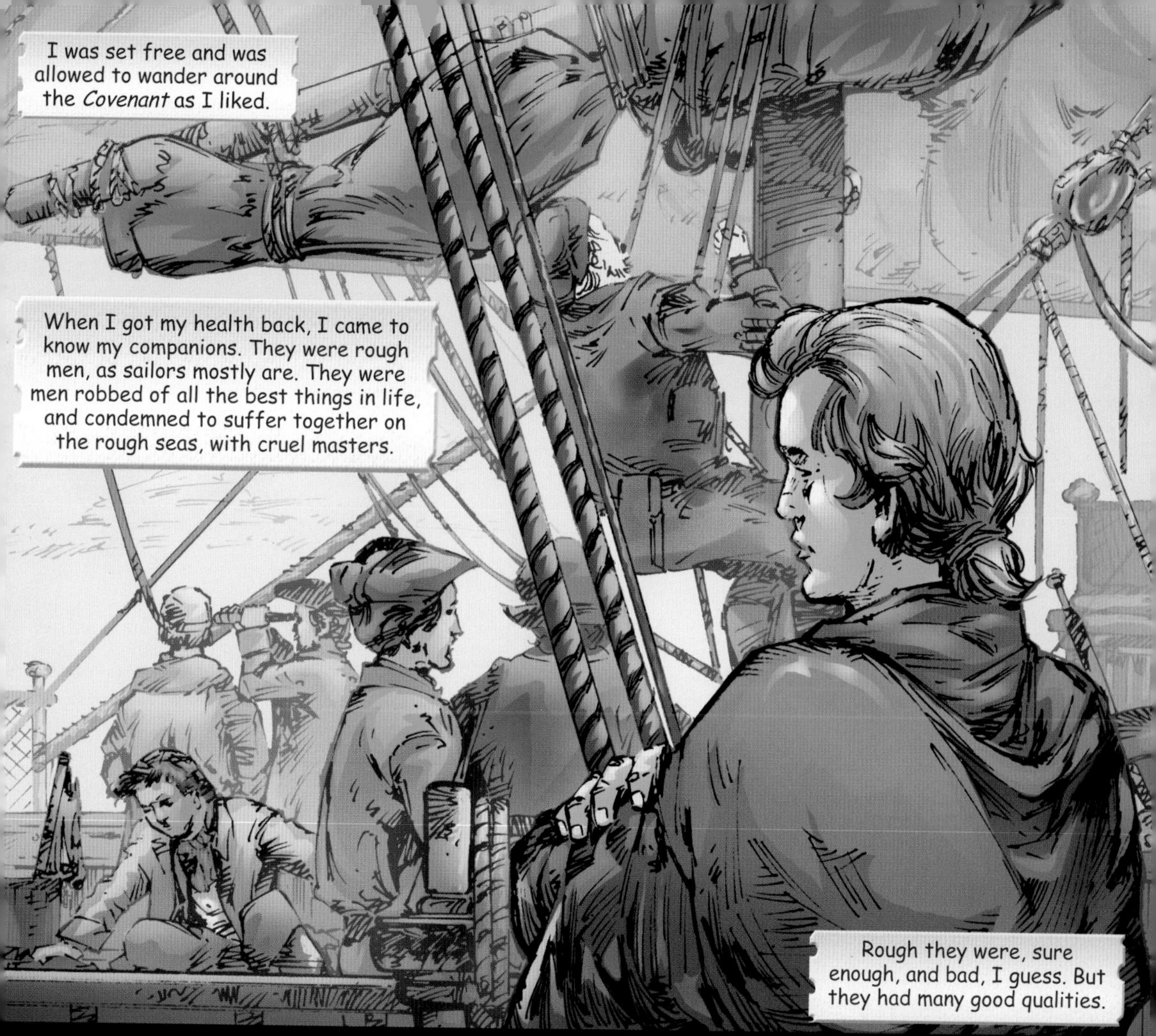
I was set free and was allowed to wander around the *Covenant* as I liked.
When I got my health back, I came to know my companions. They were rough men, as sailors mostly are. They were men robbed of all the best things in life, and condemned to suffer together on the rough seas, with cruel masters.
Rough they were, sure enough, and bad, I guess. But they had many good qualities.

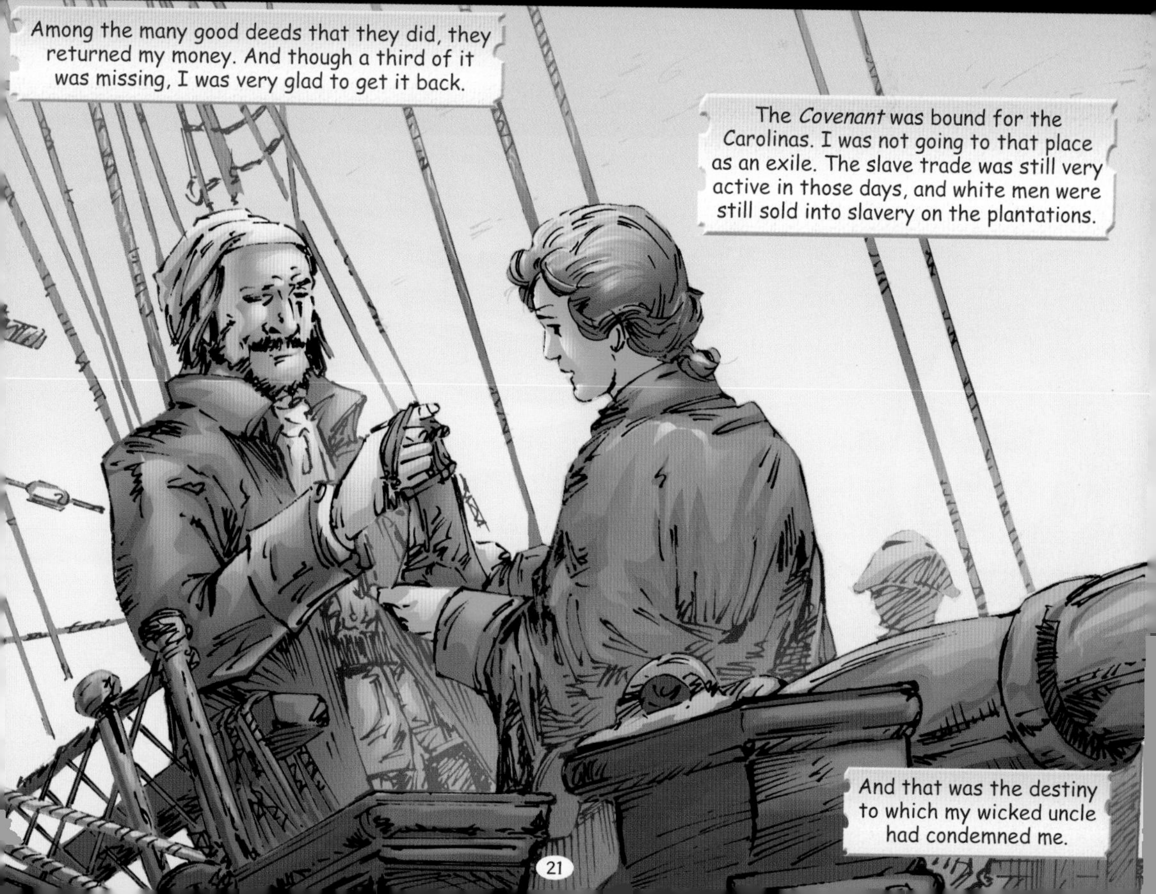
Among the many good deeds that they did, they returned my money. And though a third of it was missing, I was very glad to get it back.
The *Covenant* was bound for the Carolinas. I was not going to that place as an exile. The slave trade was still very active in those days, and white men were still sold into slavery on the plantations.
And that was the destiny to which my wicked uncle had condemned me.

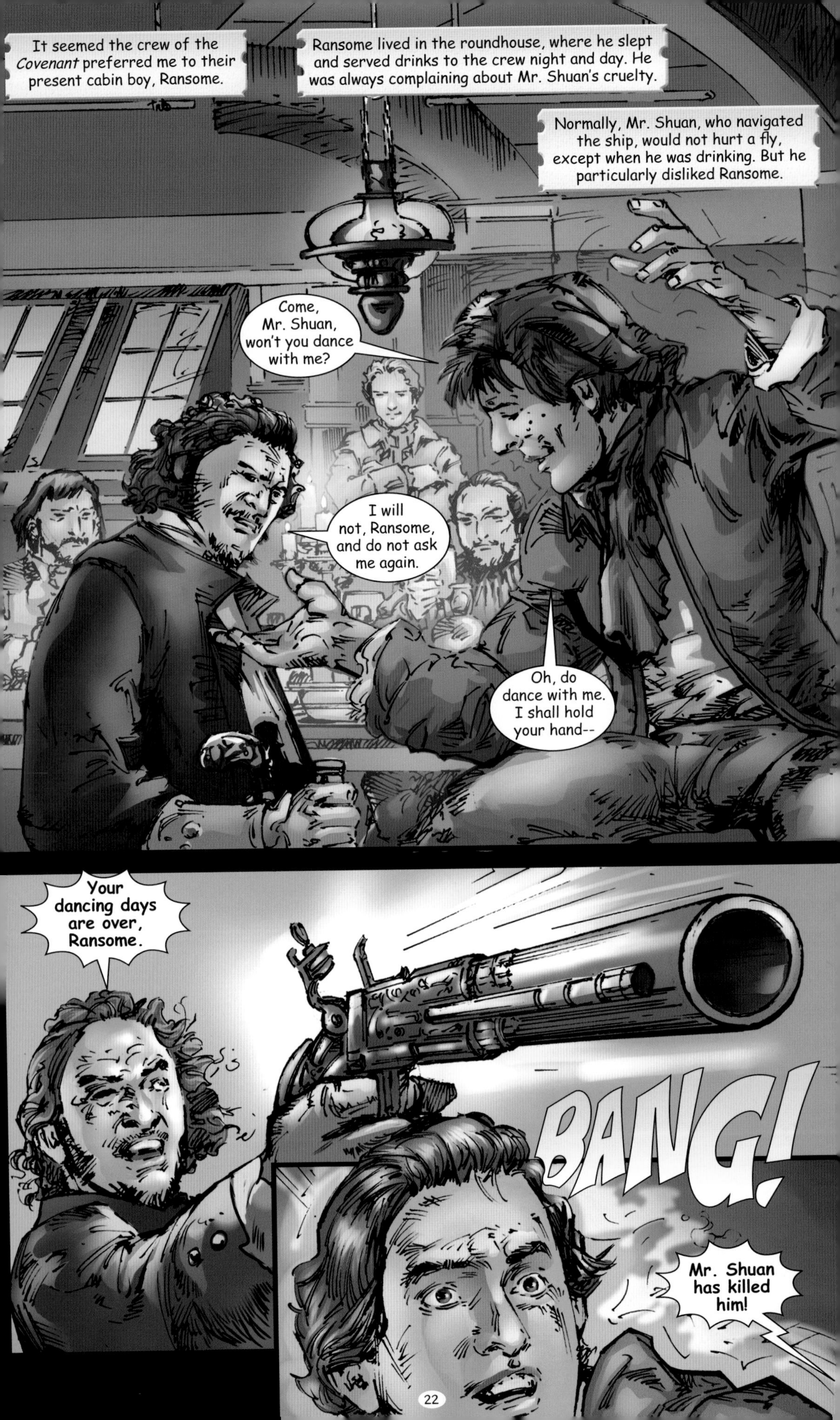

It seemed the crew of the *Covenant* preferred me to their present cabin boy, Ransome.
Ransome lived in the roundhouse, where he slept and served drinks to the crew night and day. He was always complaining about Mr. Shuan's cruelty.
Normally, Mr. Shuan, who navigated the ship, would not hurt a fly, except when he was drinking. But he particularly disliked Ransome.
Come, Mr. Shuan, won't you dance with me?
I will not, Ransome, and do not ask me again.
Oh, do dance with me. I shall hold your hand--
Your dancing days are over, Ransome.
BANG!
Mr. Shuan has killed him!

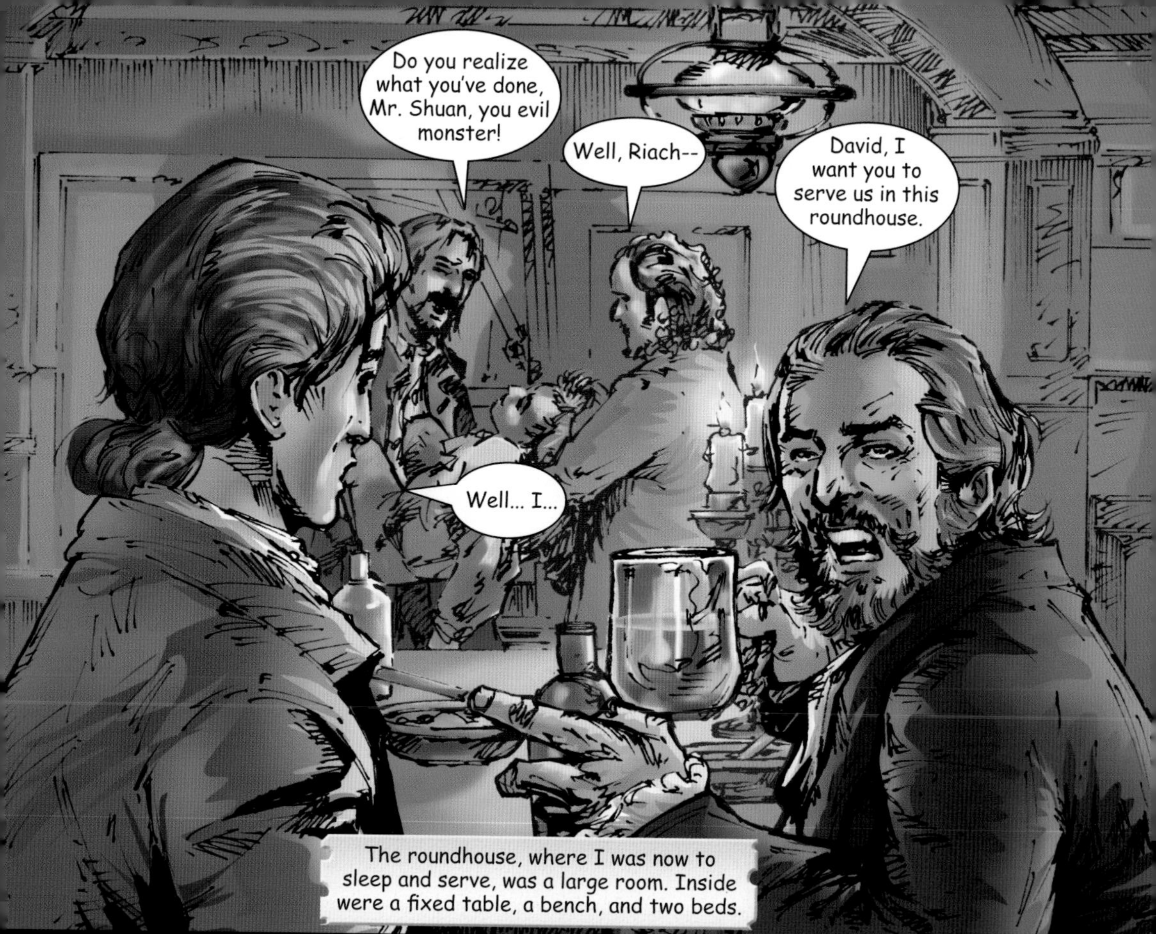
Do you realize what you've done, Mr. Shuan, you evil monster!
Well, Riach--
David, I want you to serve us in this roundhouse.
Well... I...
The roundhouse, where I was now to sleep and serve, was a large room. Inside were a fixed table, a bench, and two beds.

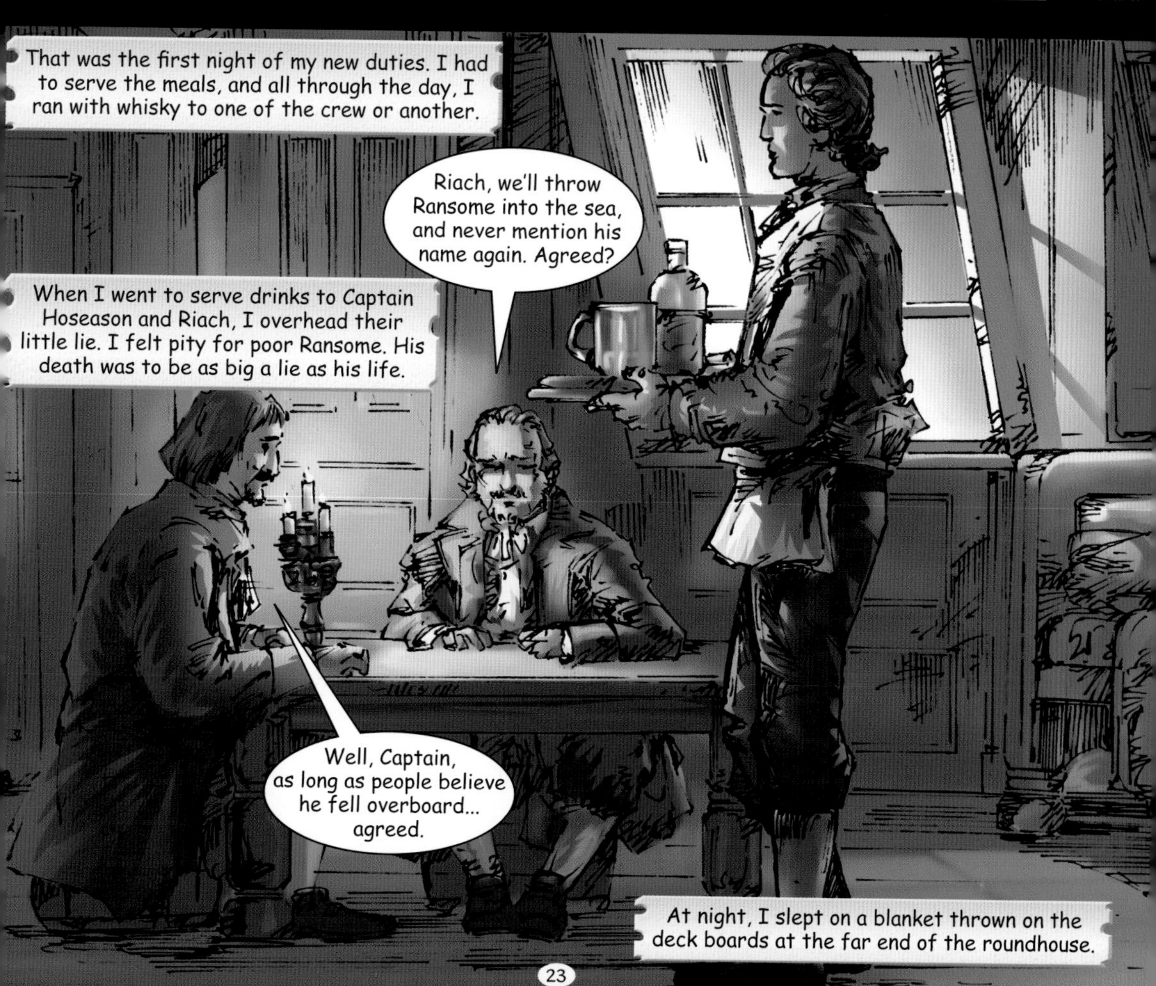
That was the first night of my new duties. I had to serve the meals, and all through the day, I ran with whisky to one of the crew or another.
Riach, we'll throw Ransome into the sea, and never mention his name again. Agreed?
When I went to serve drinks to Captain Hoseason and Riach, I overhead their little lie. I felt pity for poor Ransome. His death was to be as big a lie as his life.
Well, Captain, as long as people believe he fell overboard... agreed.
At night, I slept on a blanket thrown on the deck boards at the far end of the roundhouse.

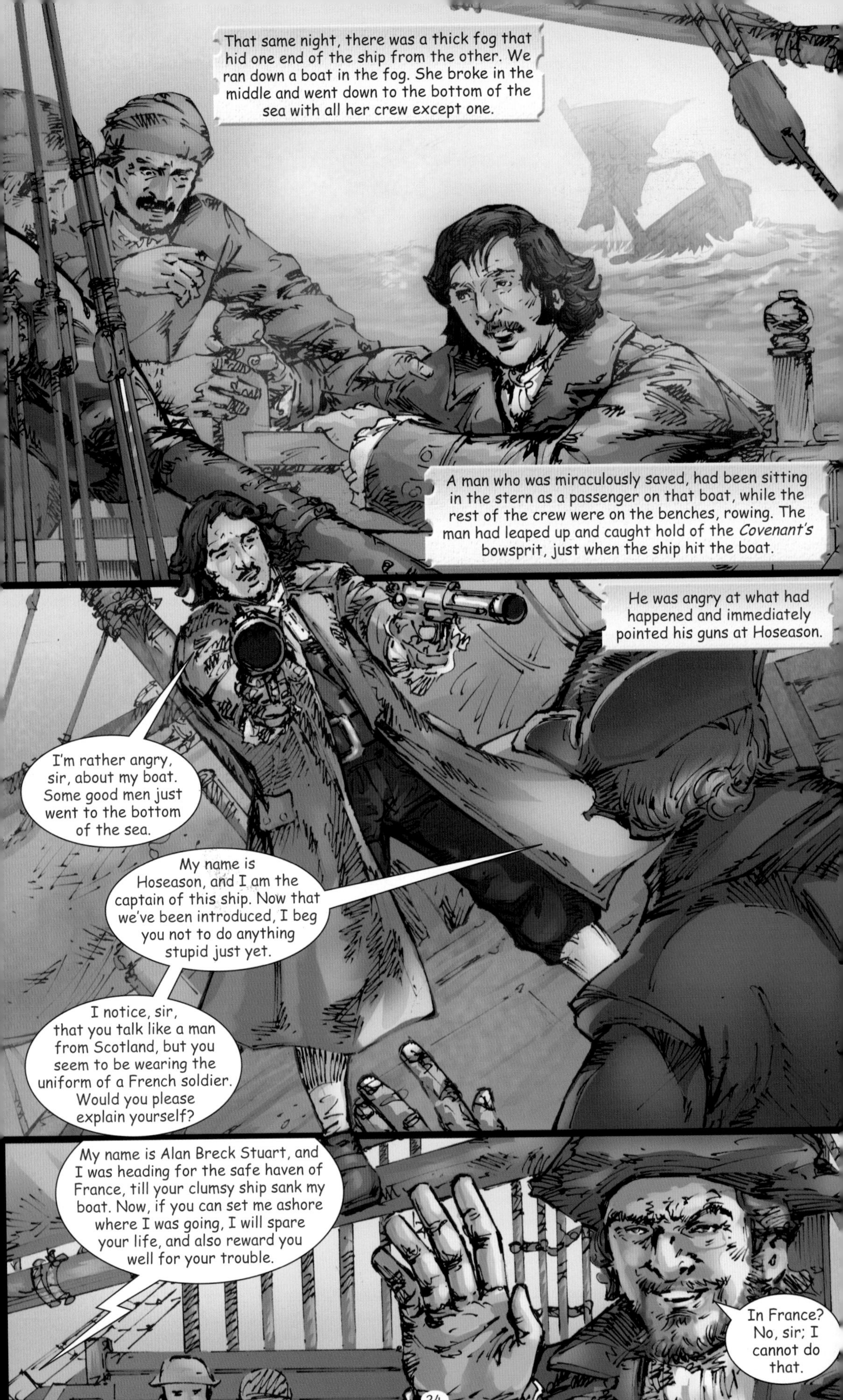

That same night, there was a thick fog that hid one end of the ship from the other. We ran down a boat in the fog. She broke in the middle and went down to the bottom of the sea with all her crew except one.
A man who was miraculously saved, had been sitting in the stern as a passenger on that boat, while the rest of the crew were on the benches, rowing. The man had leaped up and caught hold of the *Covenant's* bowsprit, just when the ship hit the boat.
He was angry at what had happened and immediately pointed his guns at Hoseason.
I'm rather angry, sir, about my boat. Some good men just went to the bottom of the sea.
My name is Hoseason, and I am the captain of this ship. Now that we've been introduced, I beg you not to do anything stupid just yet.
I notice, sir, that you talk like a man from Scotland, but you seem to be wearing the uniform of a French soldier. Would you please explain yourself?
My name is Alan Breck Stuart, and I was heading for the safe haven of France, till your clumsy ship sank my boat. Now, if you can set me ashore where I was going, I will spare your life, and also reward you well for your trouble.
In France? No, sir; I cannot do that.

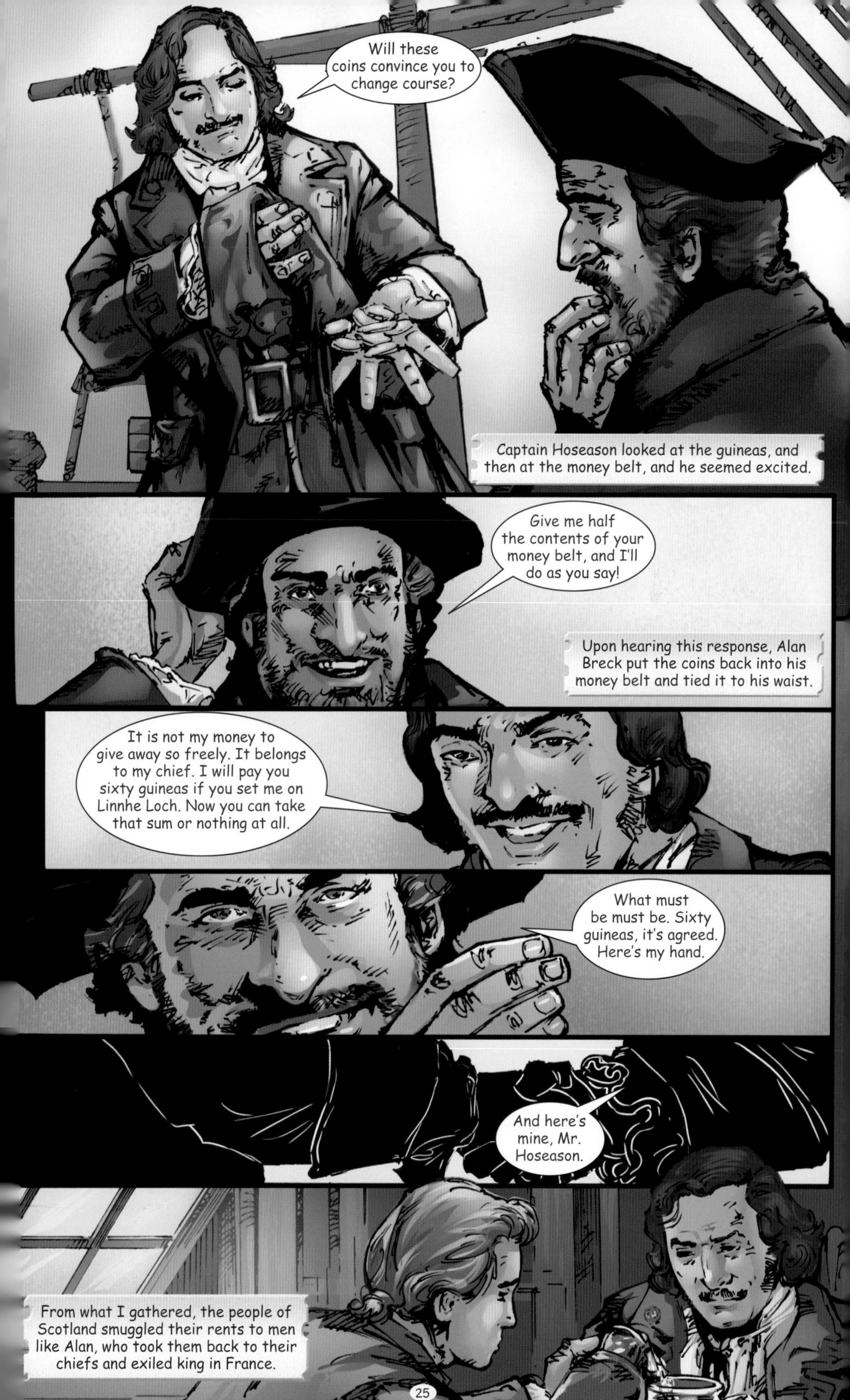

Will these coins convince you to change course?
Captain Hoseason looked at the guineas, and then at the money belt, and he seemed excited.
Give me half the contents of your money belt, and I'll do as you say!
Upon hearing this response, Alan Breck put the coins back into his money belt and tied it to his waist.
It is not my money to give away so freely. It belongs to my chief. I will pay you sixty guineas if you set me on Linnhe Loch. Now you can take that sum or nothing at all.
What must be must be. Sixty guineas, it's agreed. Here's my hand.
And here's mine, Mr. Hoseason.
From what I gathered, the people of Scotland smuggled their rents to men like Alan, who took them back to their chiefs and exiled king in France.

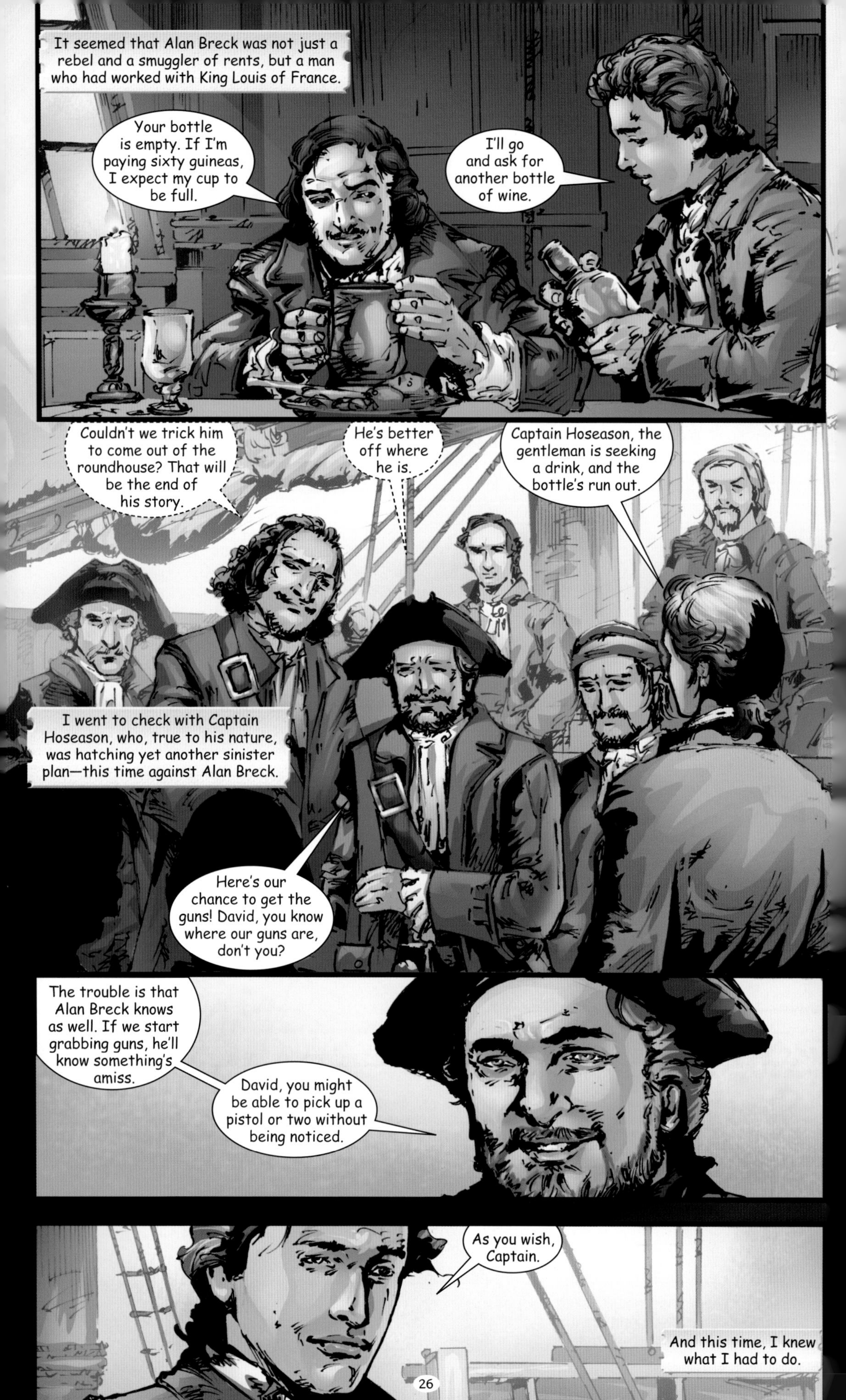
It seemed that Alan Breck was not just a rebel and a smuggler of rents, but a man who had worked with King Louis of France.
Your bottle is empty. If I'm paying sixty guineas, I expect my cup to be full.
I'll go and ask for another bottle of wine.
Couldn't we trick him to come out of the roundhouse? That will be the end of his story.
He's better off where he is.
Captain Hoseason, the gentleman is seeking a drink, and the bottle's run out.
I went to check with Captain Hoseason, who, true to his nature, was hatching yet another sinister plan—this time against Alan Breck.
Here's our chance to get the guns! David, you know where our guns are, don't you?
The trouble is that Alan Breck knows as well. If we start grabbing guns, he'll know something's amiss.
David, you might be able to pick up a pistol or two without being noticed.
As you wish, Captain.
And this time, I knew what I had to do.

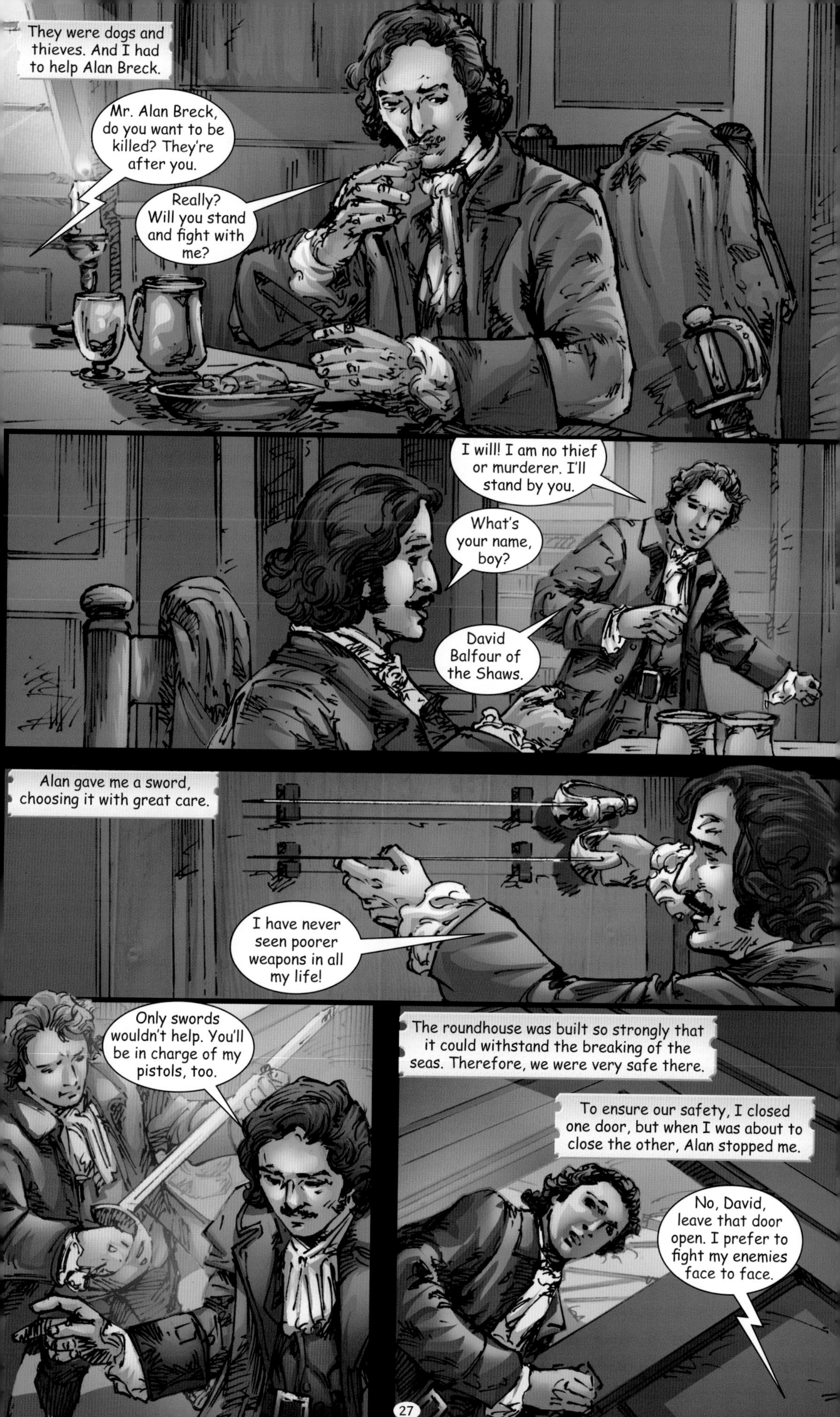
They were dogs and thieves. And I had to help Alan Breck.
Mr. Alan Breck, do you want to be killed? They're after you.
Really? Will you stand and fight with me?
I will! I am no thief or murderer. I'll stand by you.
What's your name, boy?
David Balfour of the Shaws.
Alan gave me a sword, choosing it with great care.
I have never seen poorer weapons in all my life!
Only swords wouldn't help. You'll be in charge of my pistols, too.
The roundhouse was built so strongly that it could withstand the breaking of the seas. Therefore, we were very safe there.
To ensure our safety, I closed one door, but when I was about to close the other, Alan stopped me.
No, David, leave that door open. I prefer to fight my enemies face to face.

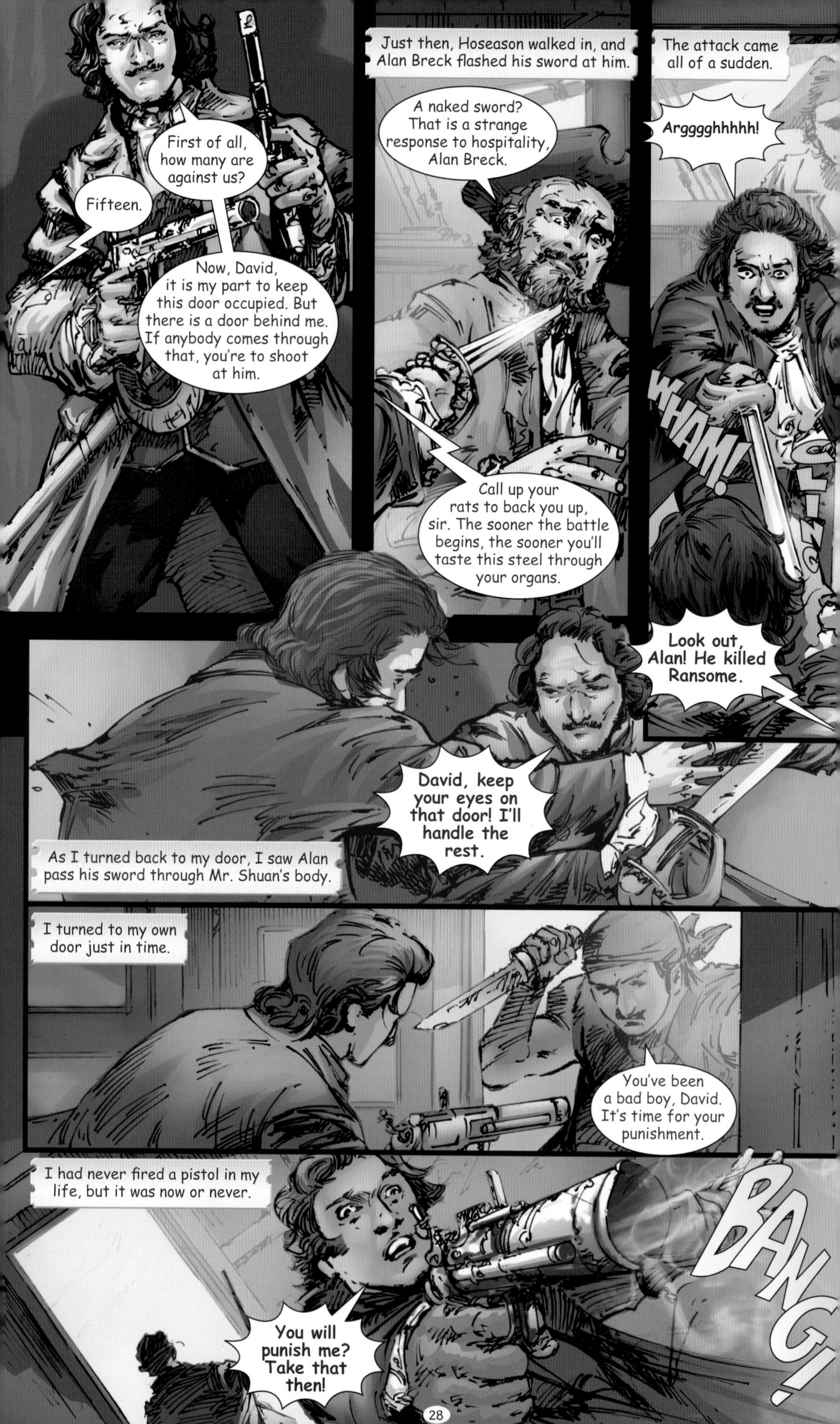
First of all, how many are against us?
Fifteen.
Now, David, it is my part to keep this door occupied. But there is a door behind me. If anybody comes through that, you're to shoot at him.
Just then, Hoseason walked in, and Alan Breck flashed his sword at him.
A naked sword? That is a strange response to hospitality, Alan Breck.
Call up your rats to back you up, sir. The sooner the battle begins, the sooner you'll taste this steel through your organs.
The attack came all of a sudden.
Arrggghhhhh!
WHAM!
Look out, Alan! He killed Ransome.
David, keep your eyes on that door! I'll handle the rest.
As I turned back to my door, I saw Alan pass his sword through Mr. Shuan's body.
I turned to my own door just in time.
You've been a bad boy, David. It's time for your punishment.
I had never fired a pistol in my life, but it was now or never.
You will punish me? Take that then!
BANG!

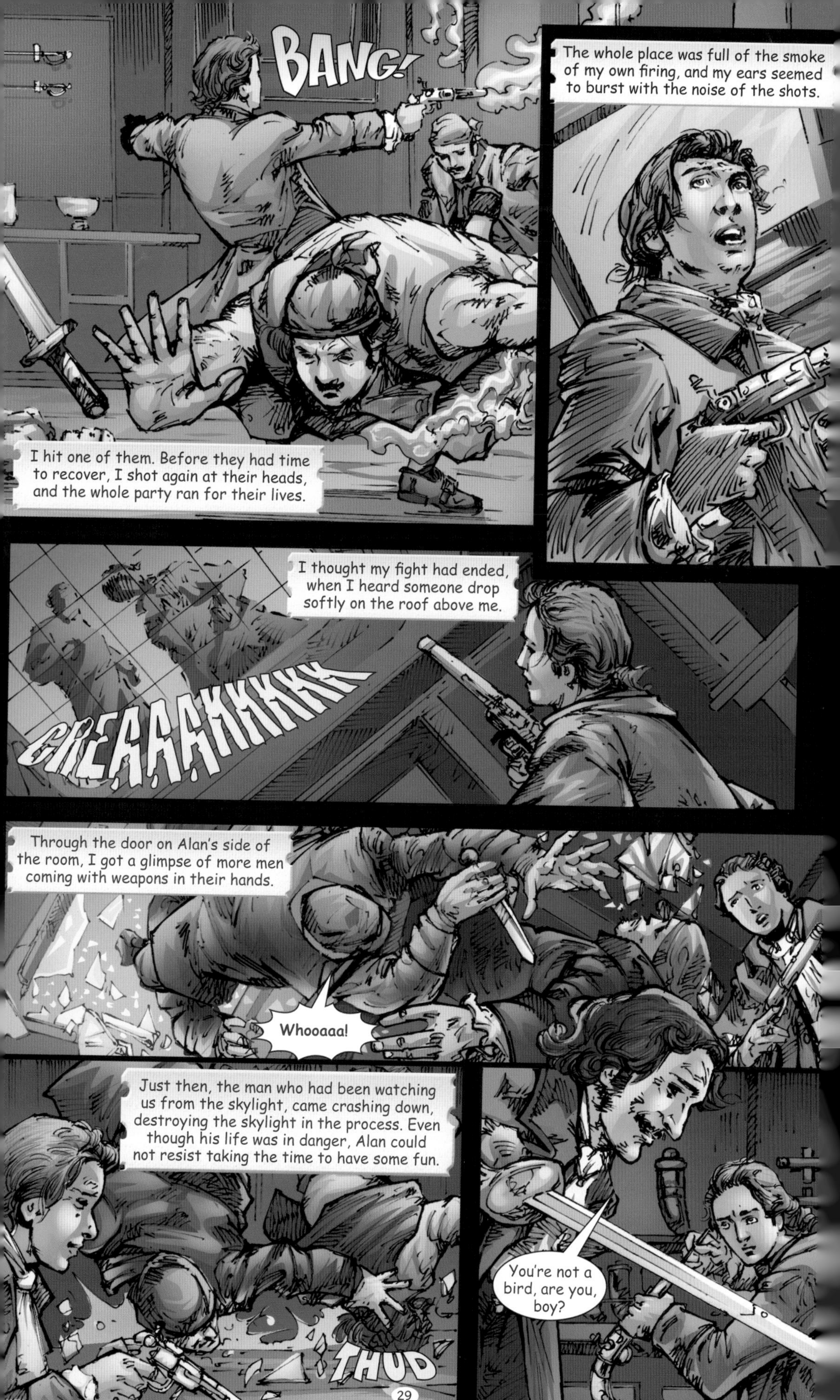

BANG!
The whole place was full of the smoke of my own firing, and my ears seemed to burst with the noise of the shots.
I hit one of them. Before they had time to recover, I shot again at their heads, and the whole party ran for their lives.
I thought my fight had ended, when I heard someone drop softly on the roof above me.
CREAAKKKKK
Through the door on Alan's side of the room, I got a glimpse of more men coming with weapons in their hands.
Whooaaa!
Just then, the man who had been watching us from the skylight, came crashing down, destroying the skylight in the process. Even though his life was in danger, Alan could not resist taking the time to have some fun.
THUD
You're not a bird, are you, boy?

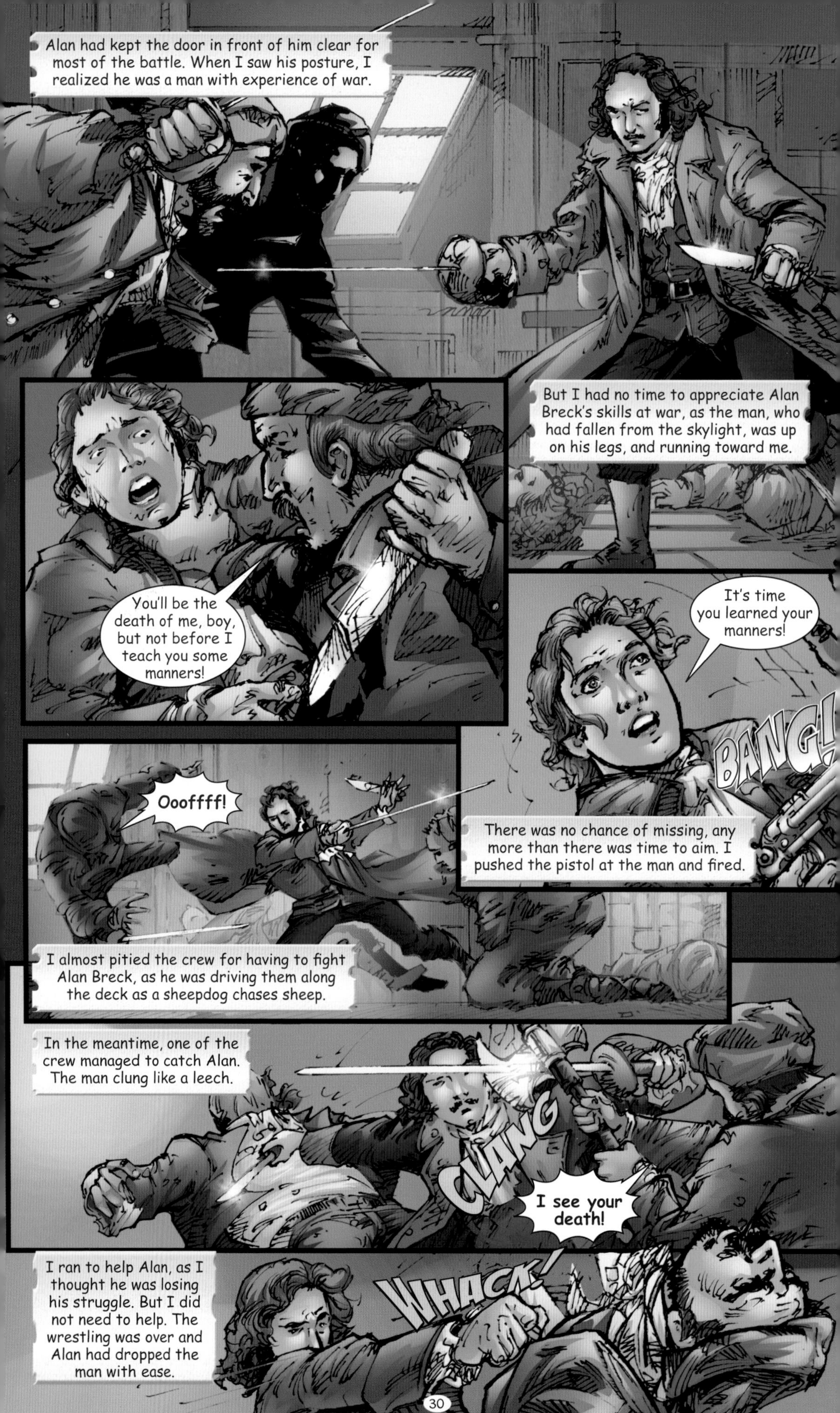
Alan had kept the door in front of him clear for most of the battle. When I saw his posture, I realized he was a man with experience of war.
But I had no time to appreciate Alan Breck's skills at war, as the man, who had fallen from the skylight, was up on his legs, and running toward me.
You'll be the death of me, boy, but not before I teach you some manners!
It's time you learned your manners!
BANG!
There was no chance of missing, any more than there was time to aim. I pushed the pistol at the man and fired.
Oooffff!
I almost pitied the crew for having to fight Alan Breck, as he was driving them along the deck as a sheepdog chases sheep.
In the meantime, one of the crew managed to catch Alan. The man clung like a leech.
CLANG
I see your death!
I ran to help Alan, as I thought he was losing his struggle. But I did not need to help. The wrestling was over and Alan had dropped the man with ease.
WHACK!

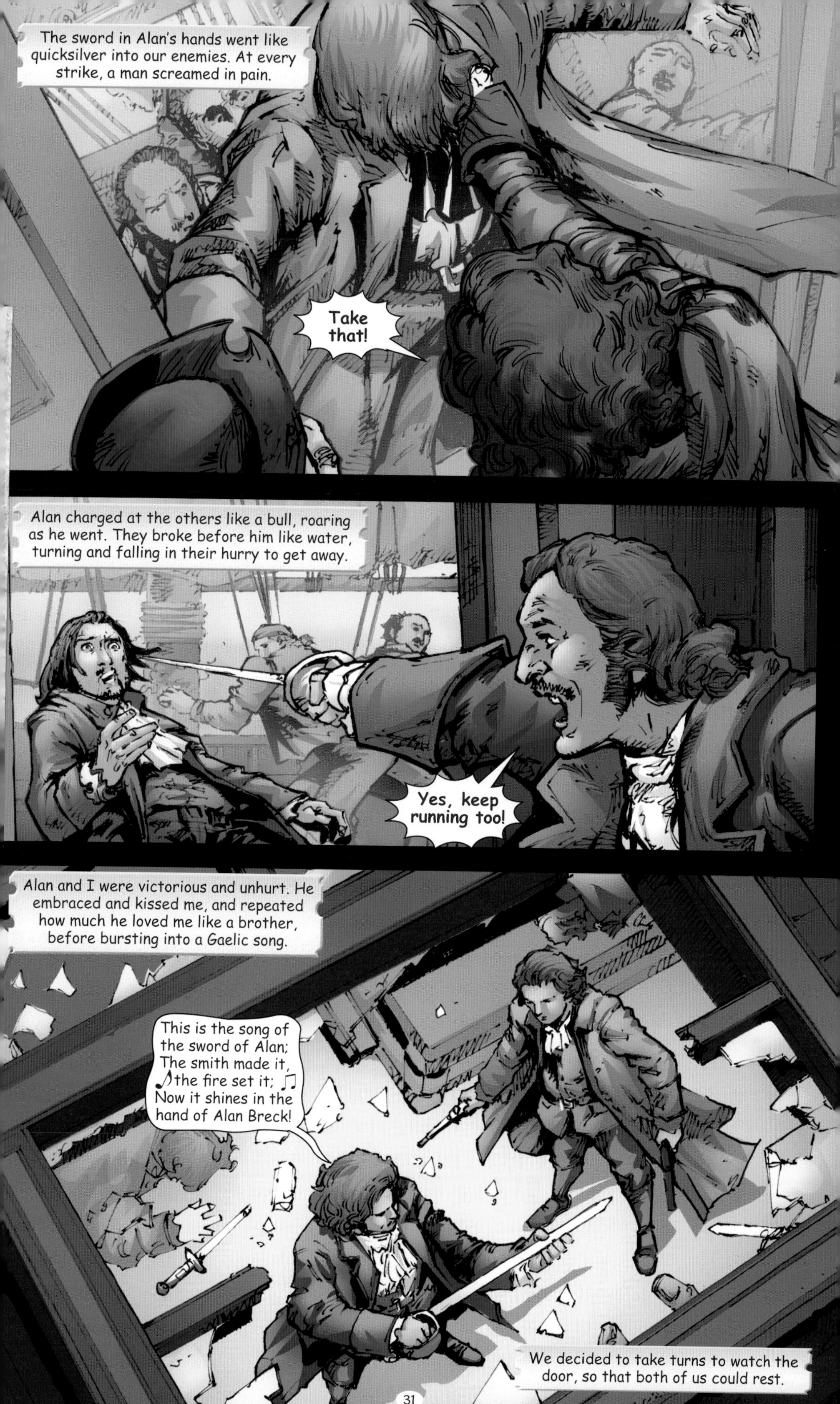

The sword in Alan's hands went like quicksilver into our enemies. At every strike, a man screamed in pain.
Take that!
Alan charged at the others like a bull, roaring as he went. They broke before him like water, turning and falling in their hurry to get away.
Yes, keep running too!
Alan and I were victorious and unhurt. He embraced and kissed me, and repeated how much he loved me like a brother, before bursting into a Gaelic song.
This is the song of the sword of Alan; The smith made it, the fire set it; Now it shines in the hand of Alan Breck!
We decided to take turns to watch the door, so that both of us could rest.

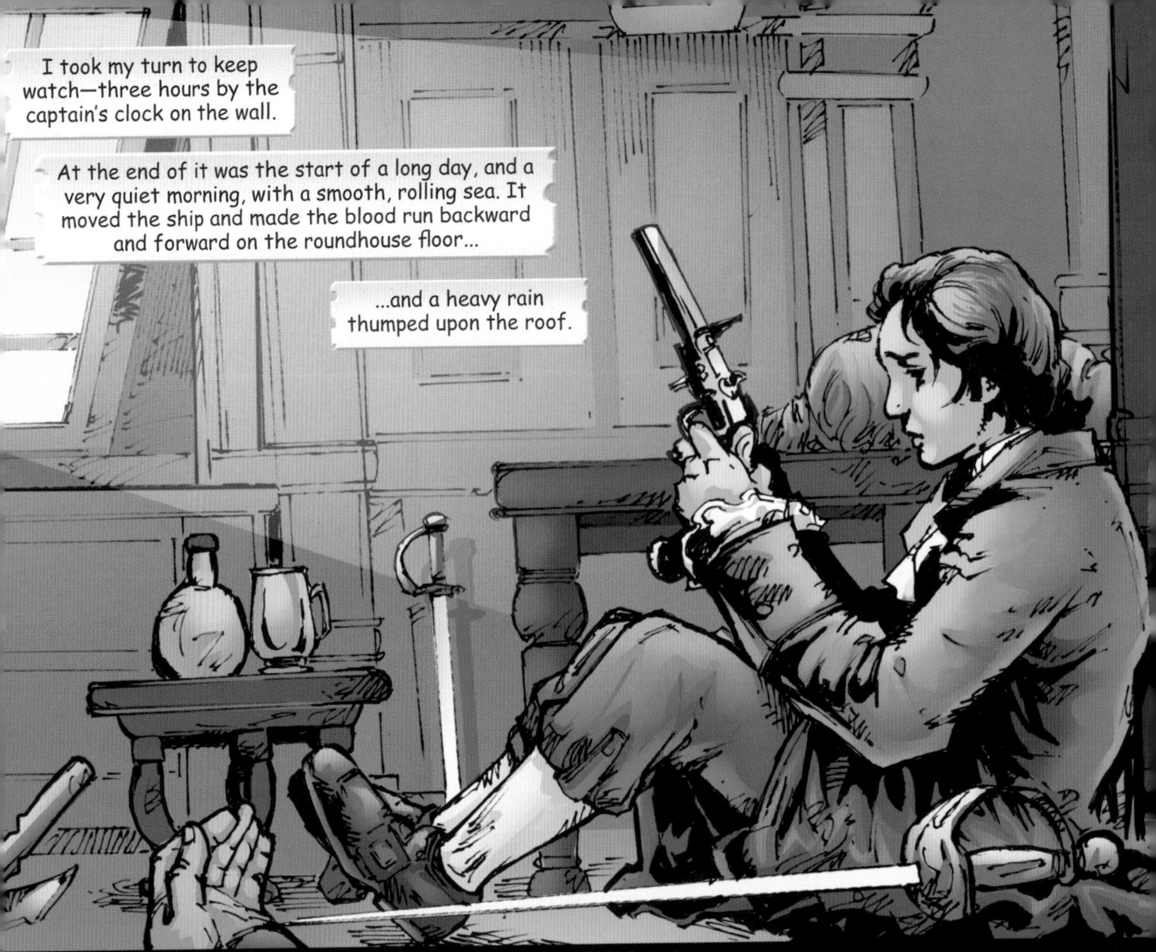
I took my turn to keep watch—three hours by the captain's clock on the wall.
At the end of it was the start of a long day, and a very quiet morning, with a smooth, rolling sea. It moved the ship and made the blood run backward and forward on the roundhouse floor...
...and a heavy rain thumped upon the roof.

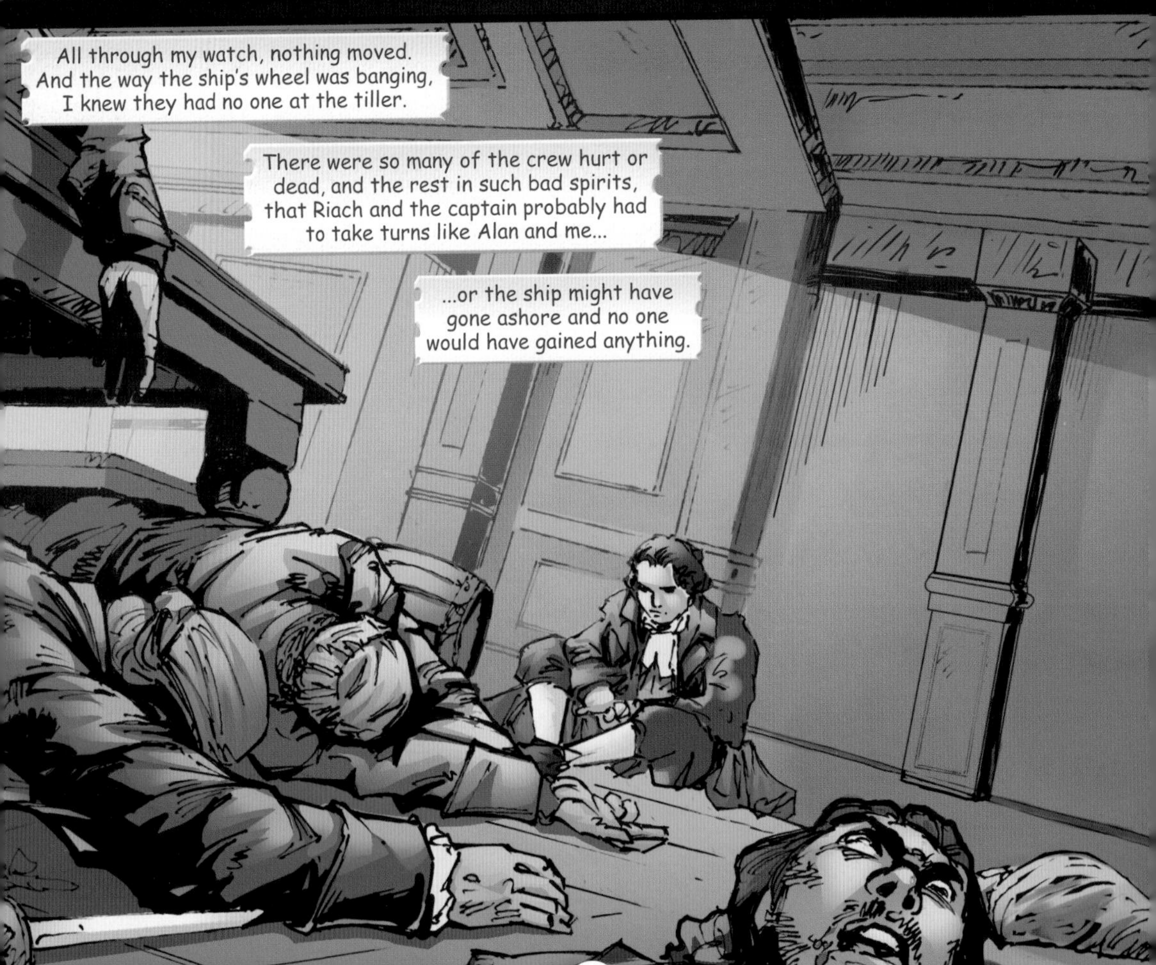
All through my watch, nothing moved. And the way the ship's wheel was banging, I knew they had no one at the tiller.
There were so many of the crew hurt or dead, and the rest in such bad spirits, that Riach and the captain probably had to take turns like Alan and me...
...or the ship might have gone ashore and no one would have gained anything.

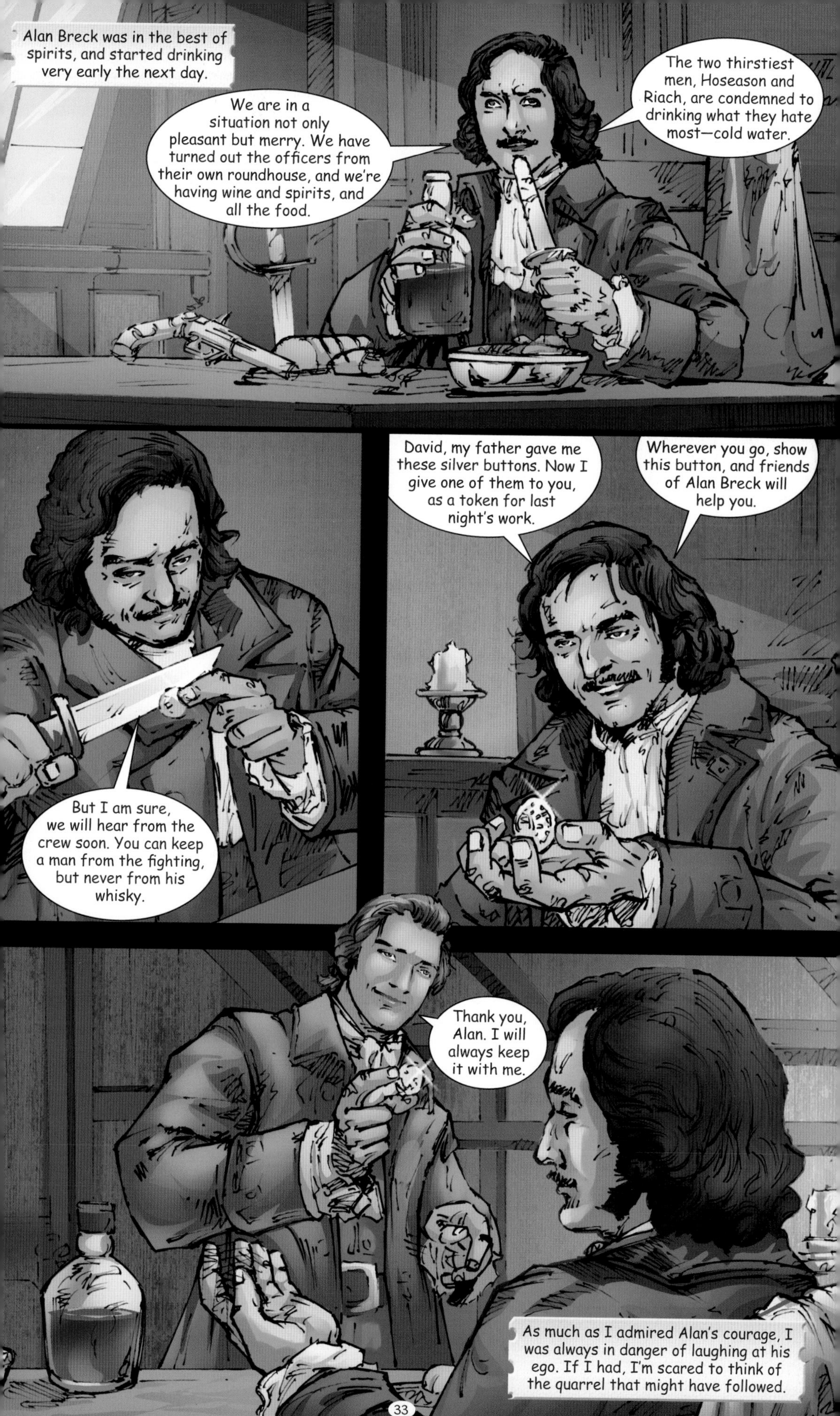
Alan Breck was in the best of spirits, and started drinking very early the next day.
We are in a situation not only pleasant but merry. We have turned out the officers from their own roundhouse, and we're having wine and spirits, and all the food.
The two thirstiest men, Hoseason and Riach, are condemned to drinking what they hate most—cold water.
But I am sure, we will hear from the crew soon. You can keep a man from the fighting, but never from his whisky.
David, my father gave me these silver buttons. Now I give one of them to you, as a token for last night's work.
Wherever you go, show this button, and friends of Alan Breck will help you.
Thank you, Alan. I will always keep it with me.
As much as I admired Alan's courage, I was always in danger of laughing at his ego. If I had, I'm scared to think of the quarrel that might have followed.

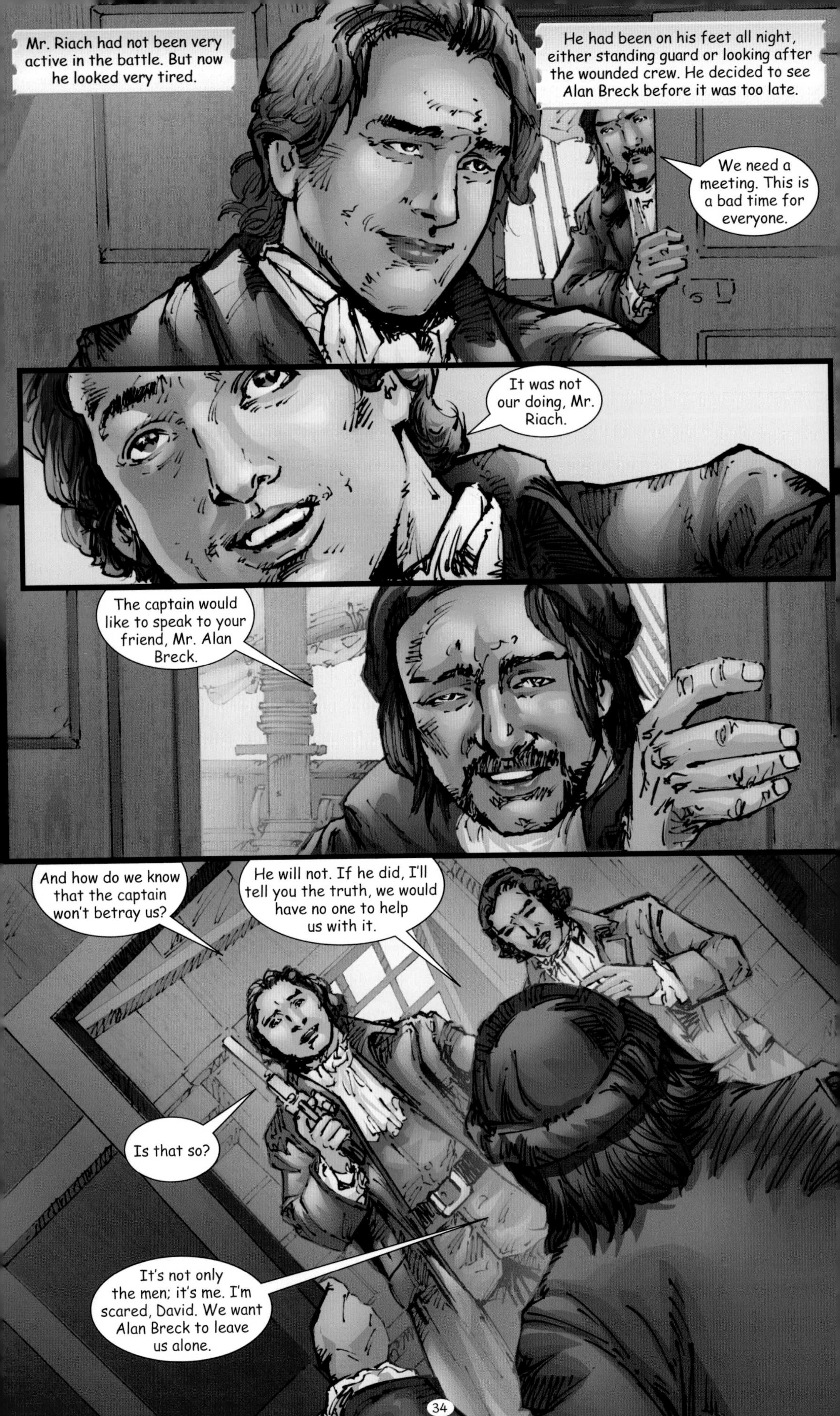
Mr. Riach had not been very active in the battle. But now he looked very tired.
He had been on his feet all night, either standing guard or looking after the wounded crew. He decided to see Alan Breck before it was too late.
We need a meeting. This is a bad time for everyone.
It was not our doing, Mr. Riach.
The captain would like to speak to your friend, Mr. Alan Breck.
And how do we know that the captain won't betray us?
He will not. If he did, I'll tell you the truth, we would have no one to help us with it.
Is that so?
It's not only the men; it's me. I'm scared, David. We want Alan Breck to leave us alone.

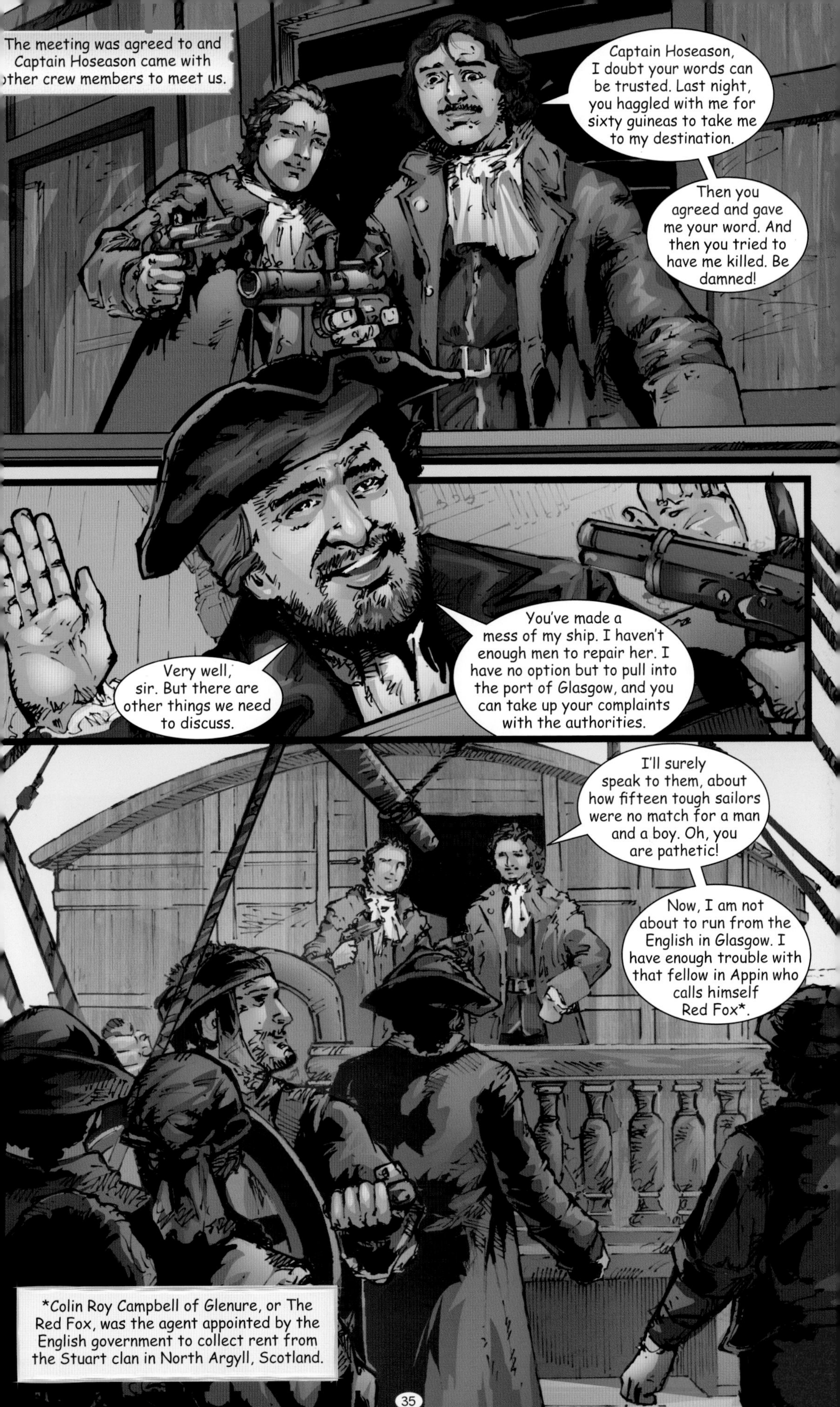

The meeting was agreed to and Captain Hoseason came with other crew members to meet us.
Captain Hoseason, I doubt your words can be trusted. Last night, you haggled with me for sixty guineas to take me to my destination.
Then you agreed and gave me your word. And then you tried to have me killed. Be damned!
Very well, sir. But there are other things we need to discuss.
You've made a mess of my ship. I haven't enough men to repair her. I have no option but to pull into the port of Glasgow, and you can take up your complaints with the authorities.
I'll surely speak to them, about how fifteen tough sailors were no match for a man and a boy. Oh, you are pathetic!
Now, I am not about to run from the English in Glasgow. I have enough trouble with that fellow in Appin who calls himself Red Fox*.
*Colin Roy Campbell of Glenure, or The Red Fox, was the agent appointed by the English government to collect rent from the Stuart clan in North Argyll, Scotland.

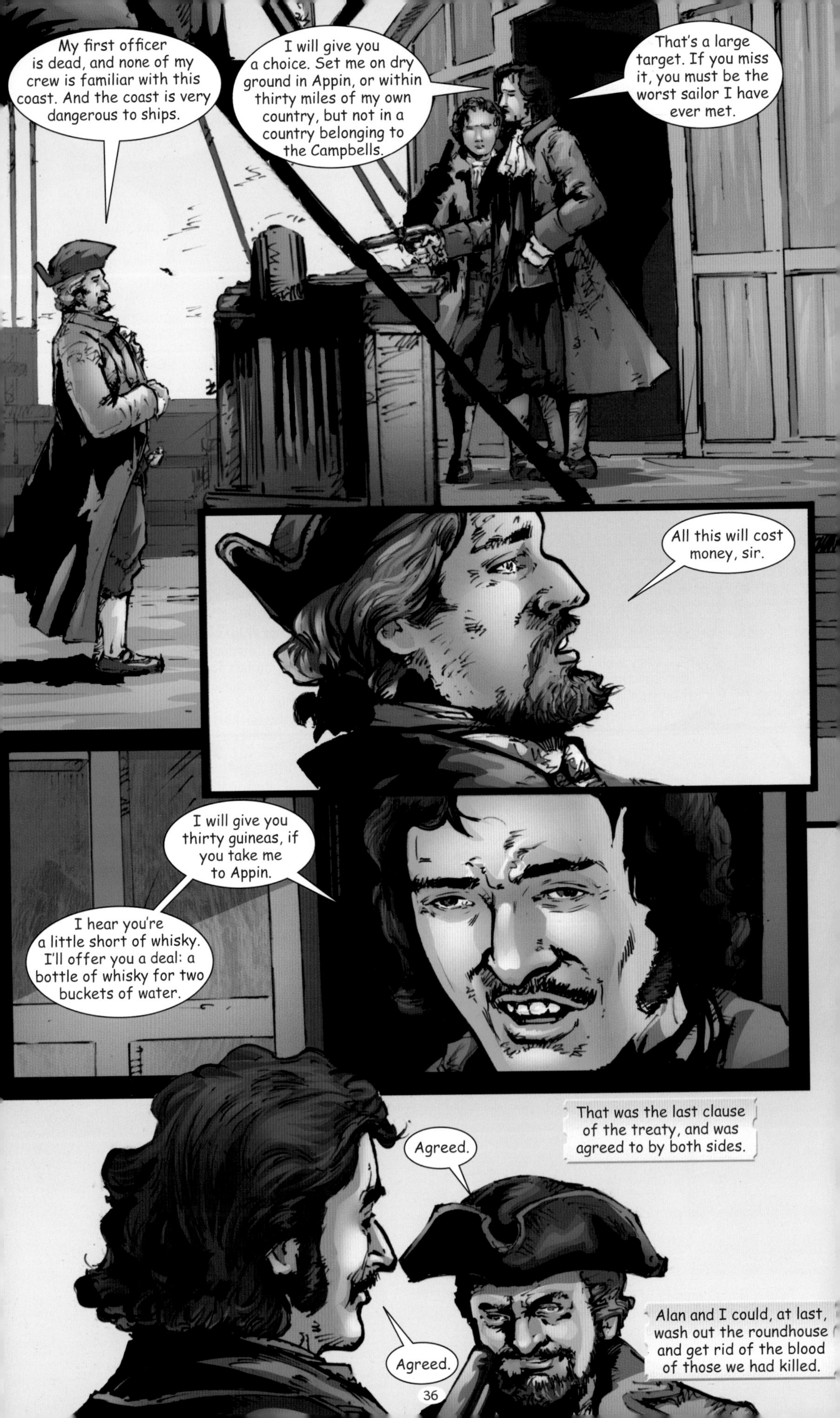
My first officer is dead, and none of my crew is familiar with this coast. And the coast is very dangerous to ships.
I will give you a choice. Set me on dry ground in Appin, or within thirty miles of my own country, but not in a country belonging to the Campbells.
That's a large target. If you miss it, you must be the worst sailor I have ever met.
All this will cost money, sir.
I will give you thirty guineas, if you take me to Appin.
I hear you're a little short of whisky. I'll offer you a deal: a bottle of whisky for two buckets of water.
That was the last clause of the treaty, and was agreed to by both sides.
Agreed.
Agreed.
Alan and I could, at last, wash out the roundhouse and get rid of the blood of those we had killed.

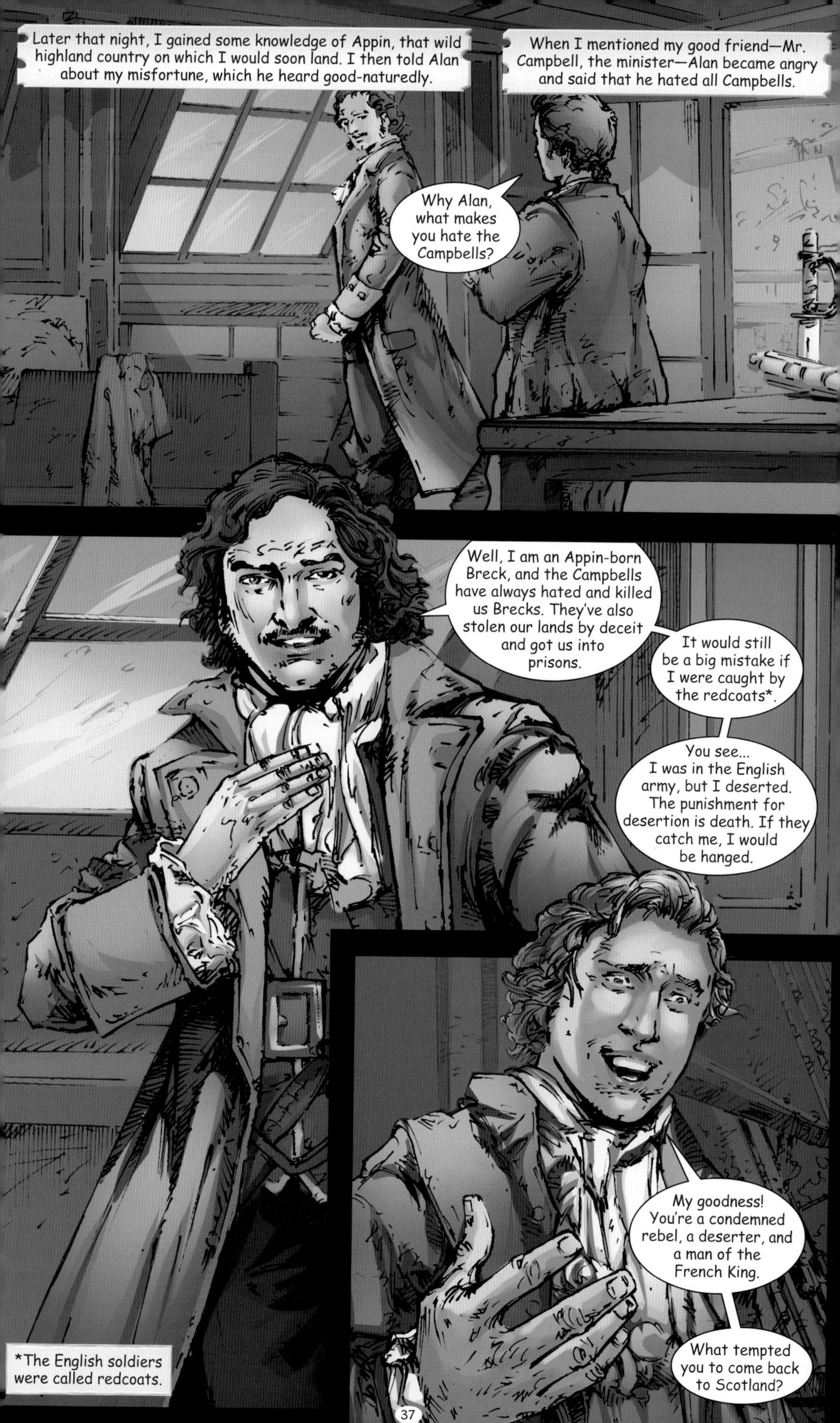
Later that night, I gained some knowledge of Appin, that wild highland country on which I would soon land. I then told Alan about my misfortune, which he heard good-naturedly.
When I mentioned my good friend—Mr. Campbell, the minister—Alan became angry and said that he hated all Campbells.
Why Alan, what makes you hate the Campbells?
Well, I am an Appin-born Breck, and the Campbells have always hated and killed us Brecks. They've also stolen our lands by deceit and got us into prisons.
It would still be a big mistake if I were caught by the redcoats*.
You see... I was in the English army, but I deserted. The punishment for desertion is death. If they catch me, I would be hanged.
My goodness! You're a condemned rebel, a deserter, and a man of the French King.
What tempted you to come back to Scotland?

*The English soldiers were called redcoats.

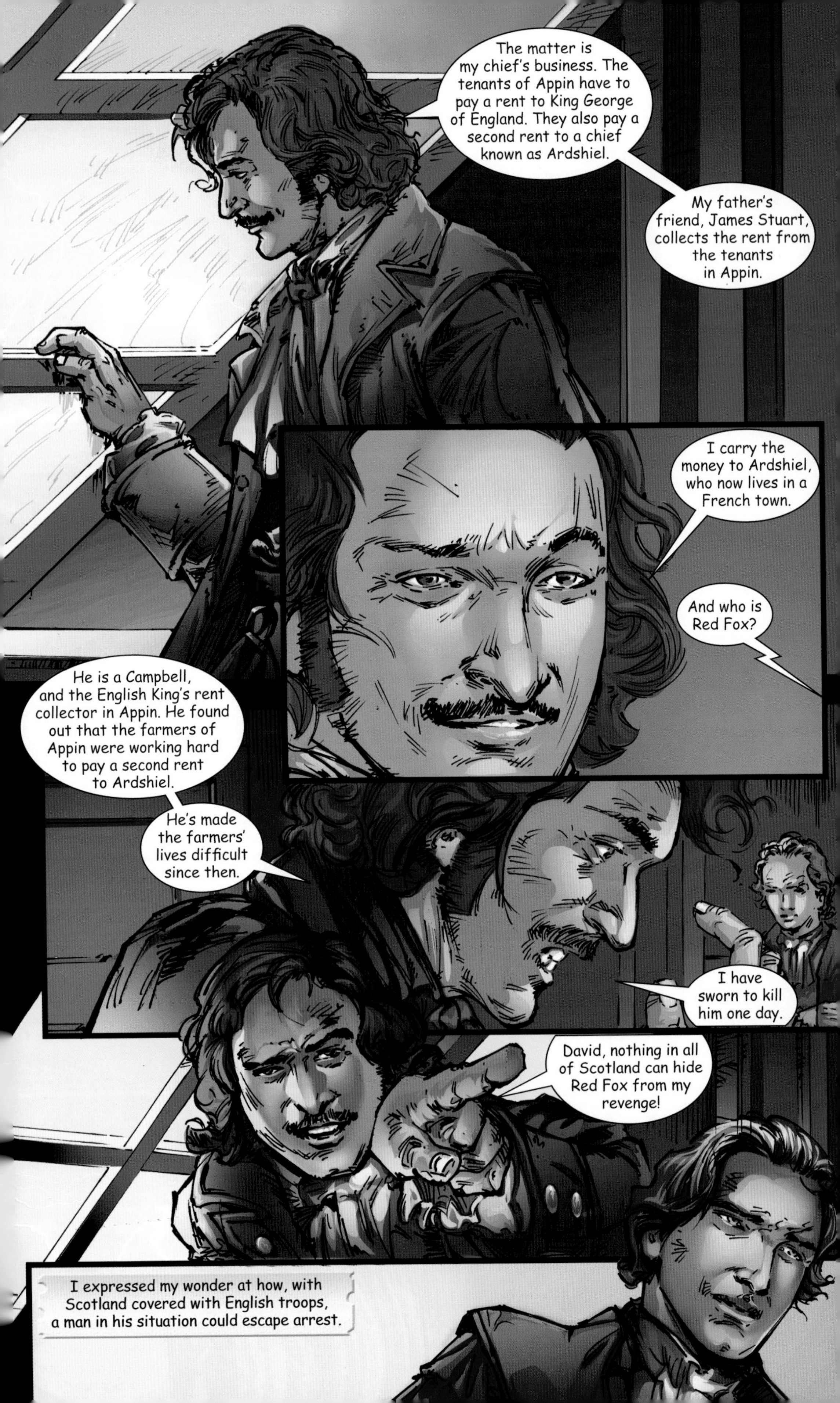
The matter is my chief's business. The tenants of Appin have to pay a rent to King George of England. They also pay a second rent to a chief known as Ardshiel.
My father's friend, James Stuart, collects the rent from the tenants in Appin.
I carry the money to Ardshiel, who now lives in a French town.
And who is Red Fox?
He is a Campbell, and the English King's rent collector in Appin. He found out that the farmers of Appin were working hard to pay a second rent to Ardshiel.
He's made the farmers' lives difficult since then.
I have sworn to kill him one day.
David, nothing in all of Scotland can hide Red Fox from my revenge!
I expressed my wonder at how, with Scotland covered with English troops, a man in his situation could escape arrest.

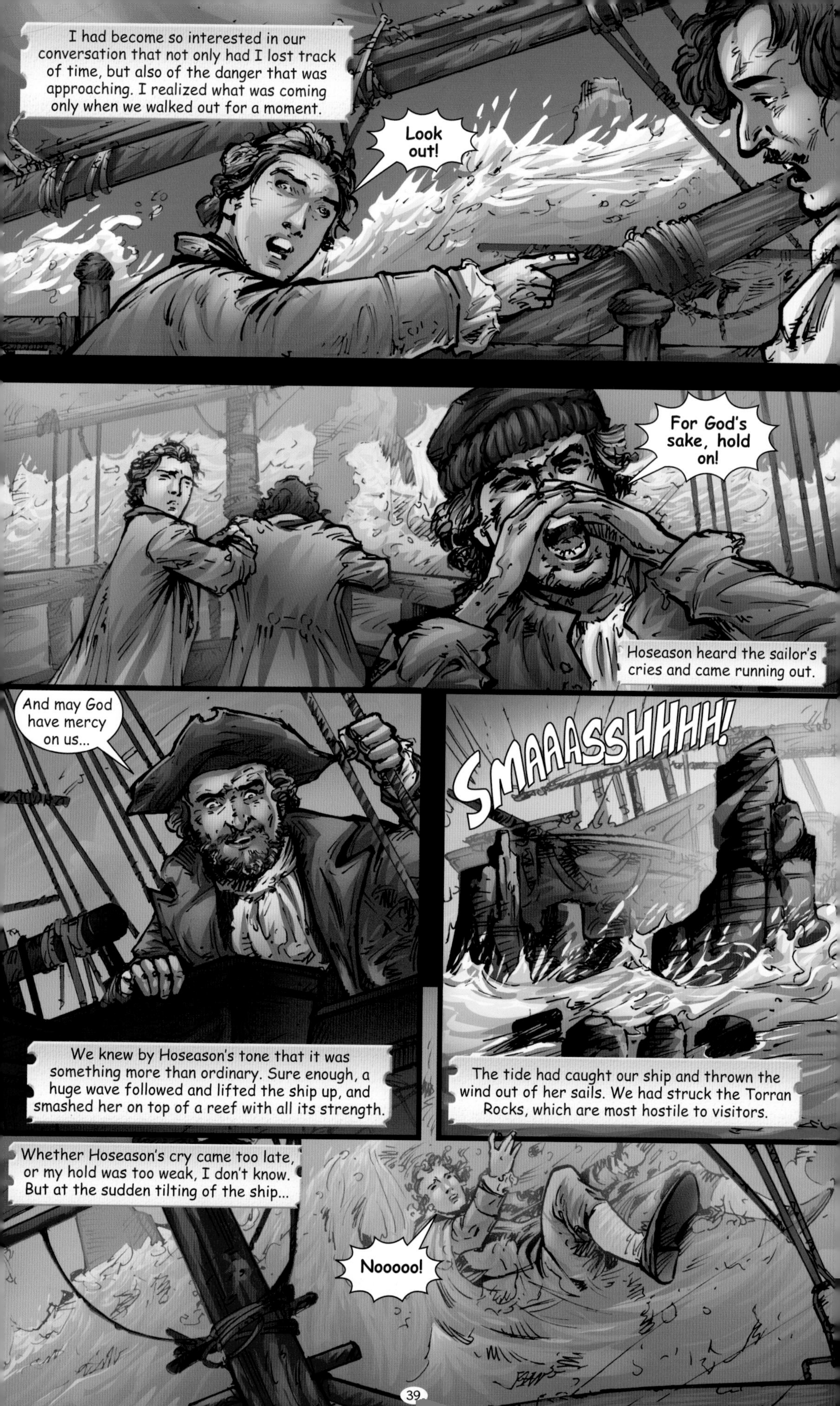
I had become so interested in our conversation that not only had I lost track of time, but also of the danger that was approaching. I realized what was coming only when we walked out for a moment.
Look out!
For God's sake, hold on!
Hoseason heard the sailor's cries and came running out.
And may God have mercy on us...
We knew by Hoseason's tone that it was something more than ordinary. Sure enough, a huge wave followed and lifted the ship up, and smashed her on top of a reef with all its strength.
SMAAASSHHHH!
The tide had caught our ship and thrown the wind out of her sails. We had struck the Torran Rocks, which are most hostile to visitors.
Whether Hoseason's cry came too late, or my hold was too weak, I don't know. But at the sudden tilting of the ship...
Nooooo!

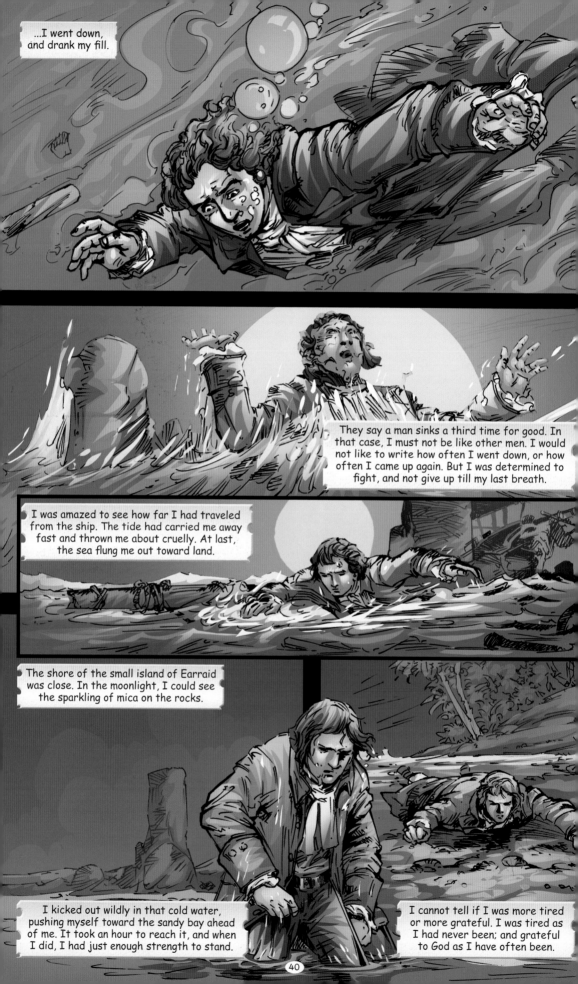

...I went down, and drank my fill.

They say a man sinks a third time for good. In that case, I must not be like other men. I would not like to write how often I went down, or how often I came up again. But I was determined to fight, and not give up till my last breath.

I was amazed to see how far I had traveled from the ship. The tide had carried me away fast and thrown me about cruelly. At last, the sea flung me out toward land.

The shore of the small island of Earraid was close. In the moonlight, I could see the sparkling of mica on the rocks.

I kicked out wildly in that cold water, pushing myself toward the sandy bay ahead of me. It took an hour to reach it, and when I did, I had just enough strength to stand.

I cannot tell if I was more tired or more grateful. I was tired as I had never been; and grateful to God as I have often been.

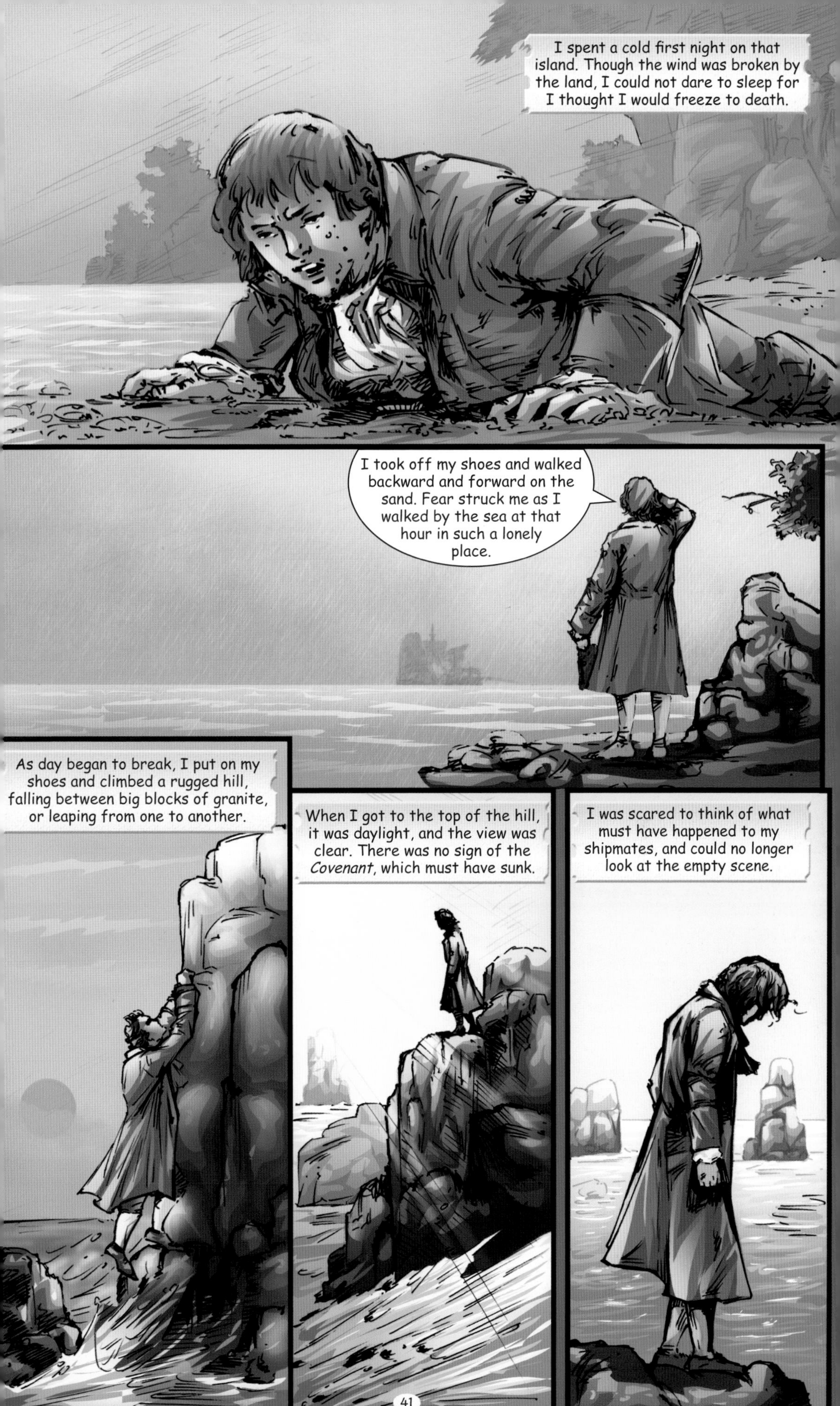
I spent a cold first night on that island. Though the wind was broken by the land, I could not dare to sleep for I thought I would freeze to death.
I took off my shoes and walked backward and forward on the sand. Fear struck me as I walked by the sea at that hour in such a lonely place.
As day began to break, I put on my shoes and climbed a rugged hill, falling between big blocks of granite, or leaping from one to another.
When I got to the top of the hill, it was daylight, and the view was clear. There was no sign of the *Covenant*, which must have sunk.
I was scared to think of what must have happened to my shipmates, and could no longer look at the empty scene.

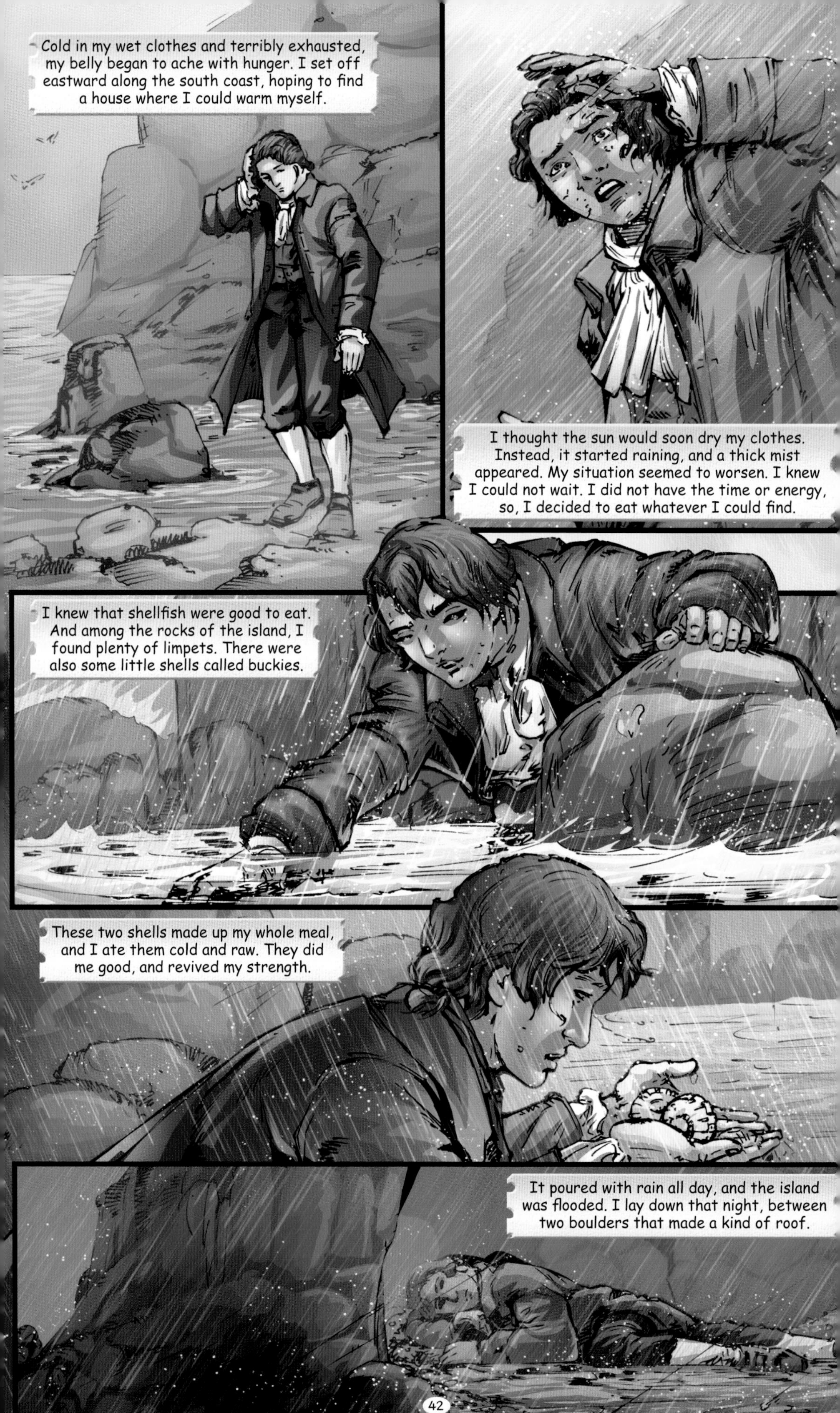
Cold in my wet clothes and terribly exhausted, my belly began to ache with hunger. I set off eastward along the south coast, hoping to find a house where I could warm myself.
I thought the sun would soon dry my clothes. Instead, it started raining, and a thick mist appeared. My situation seemed to worsen. I knew I could not wait. I did not have the time or energy, so, I decided to eat whatever I could find.
I knew that shellfish were good to eat. And among the rocks of the island, I found plenty of limpets. There were also some little shells called buckies.
These two shells made up my whole meal, and I ate them cold and raw. They did me good, and revived my strength.
It poured with rain all day, and the island was flooded. I lay down that night, between two boulders that made a kind of roof.

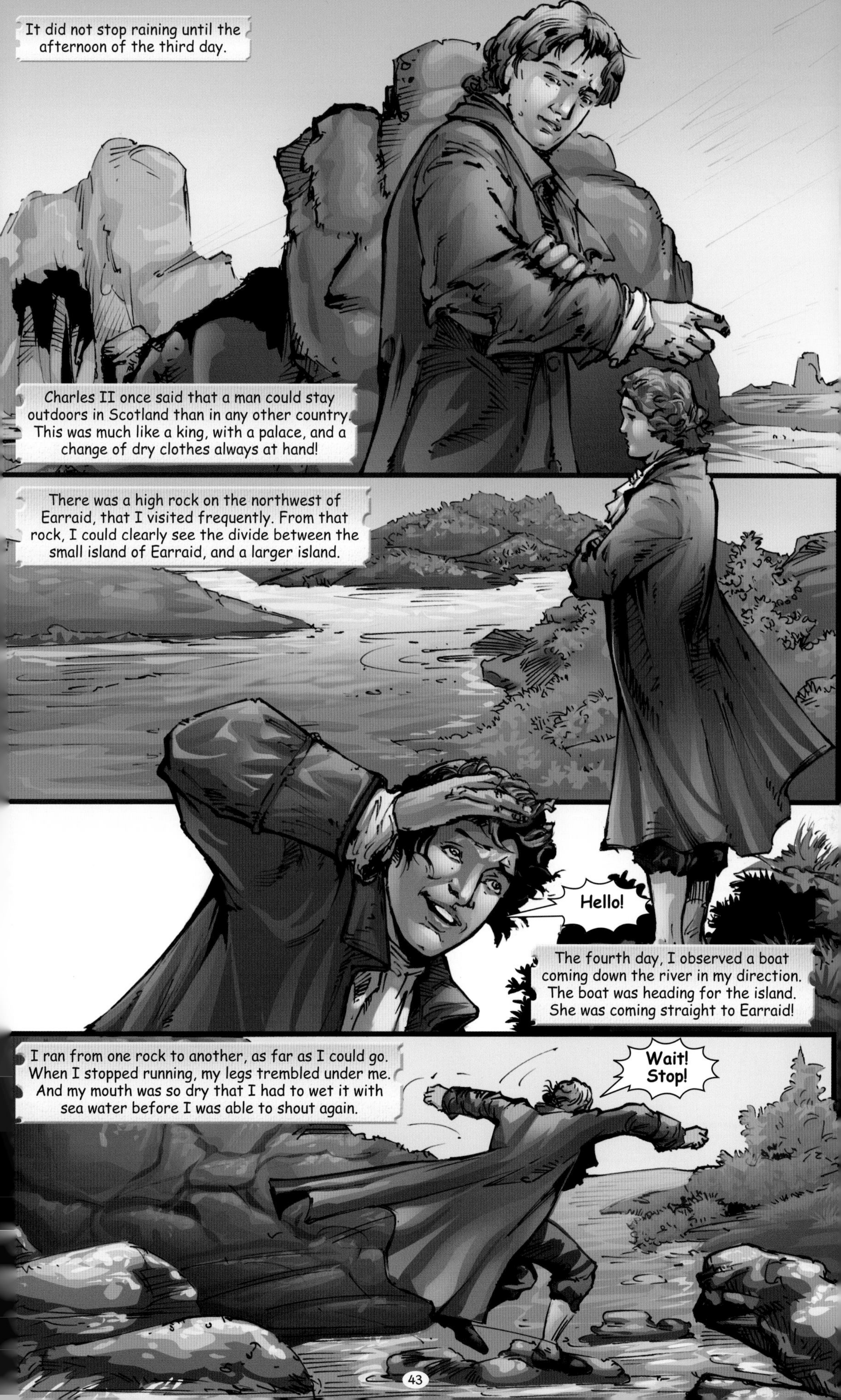
It did not stop raining until the afternoon of the third day.
Charles II once said that a man could stay outdoors in Scotland than in any other country. This was much like a king, with a palace, and a change of dry clothes always at hand!
There was a high rock on the northwest of Earraid, that I visited frequently. From that rock, I could clearly see the divide between the small island of Earraid, and a larger island.
Hello!
The fourth day, I observed a boat coming down the river in my direction. The boat was heading for the island. She was coming straight to Earraid!
I ran from one rock to another, as far as I could go. When I stopped running, my legs trembled under me. And my mouth was so dry that I had to wet it with sea water before I was able to shout again.
Wait! Stop!

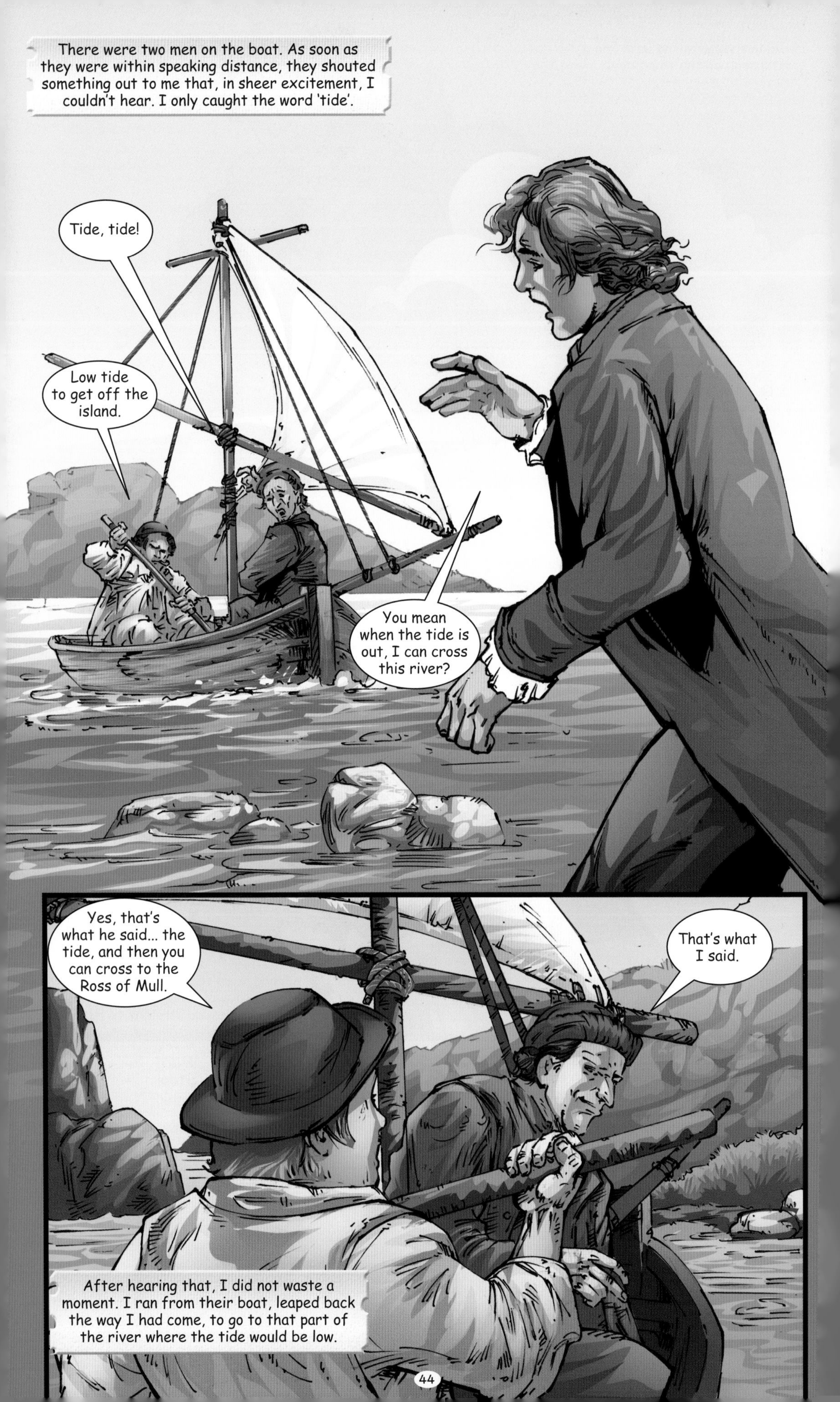
There were two men on the boat. As soon as they were within speaking distance, they shouted something out to me that, in sheer excitement, I couldn't hear. I only caught the word 'tide'.
Tide, tide!
Low tide to get off the island.
You mean when the tide is out, I can cross this river?
Yes, that's what he said... the tide, and then you can cross to the Ross of Mull.
That's what I said.
After hearing that, I did not waste a moment. I ran from their boat, leaped back the way I had come, to go to that part of the river where the tide would be low.

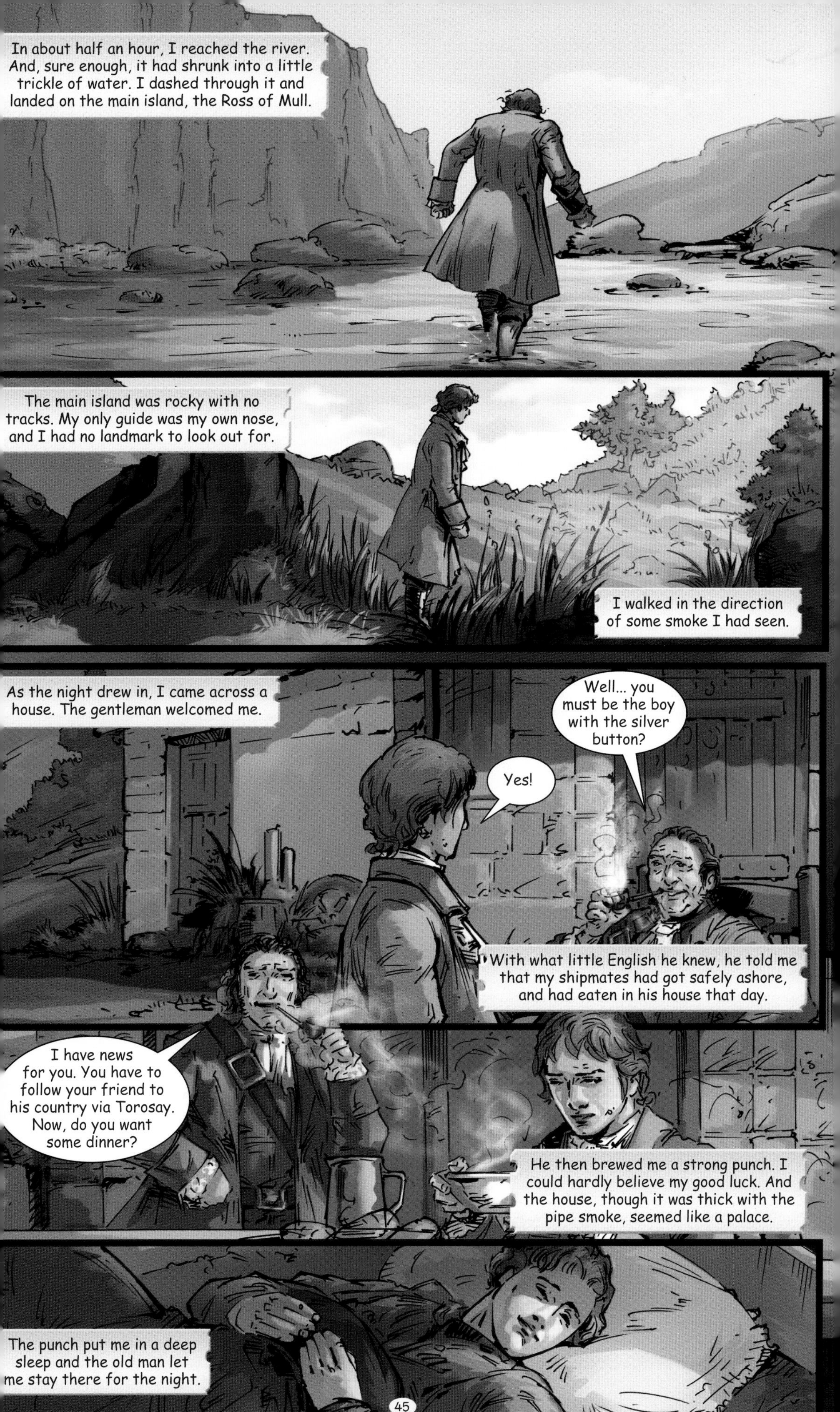

In about half an hour, I reached the river. And, sure enough, it had shrunk into a little trickle of water. I dashed through it and landed on the main island, the Ross of Mull.
The main island was rocky with no tracks. My only guide was my own nose, and I had no landmark to look out for.
I walked in the direction of some smoke I had seen.
As the night drew in, I came across a house. The gentleman welcomed me.
Well... you must be the boy with the silver button?
Yes!
With what little English he knew, he told me that my shipmates had got safely ashore, and had eaten in his house that day.
I have news for you. You have to follow your friend to his country via Torosay. Now, do you want some dinner?
He then brewed me a strong punch. I could hardly believe my good luck. And the house, though it was thick with the pipe smoke, seemed like a palace.
The punch put me in a deep sleep and the old man let me stay there for the night.

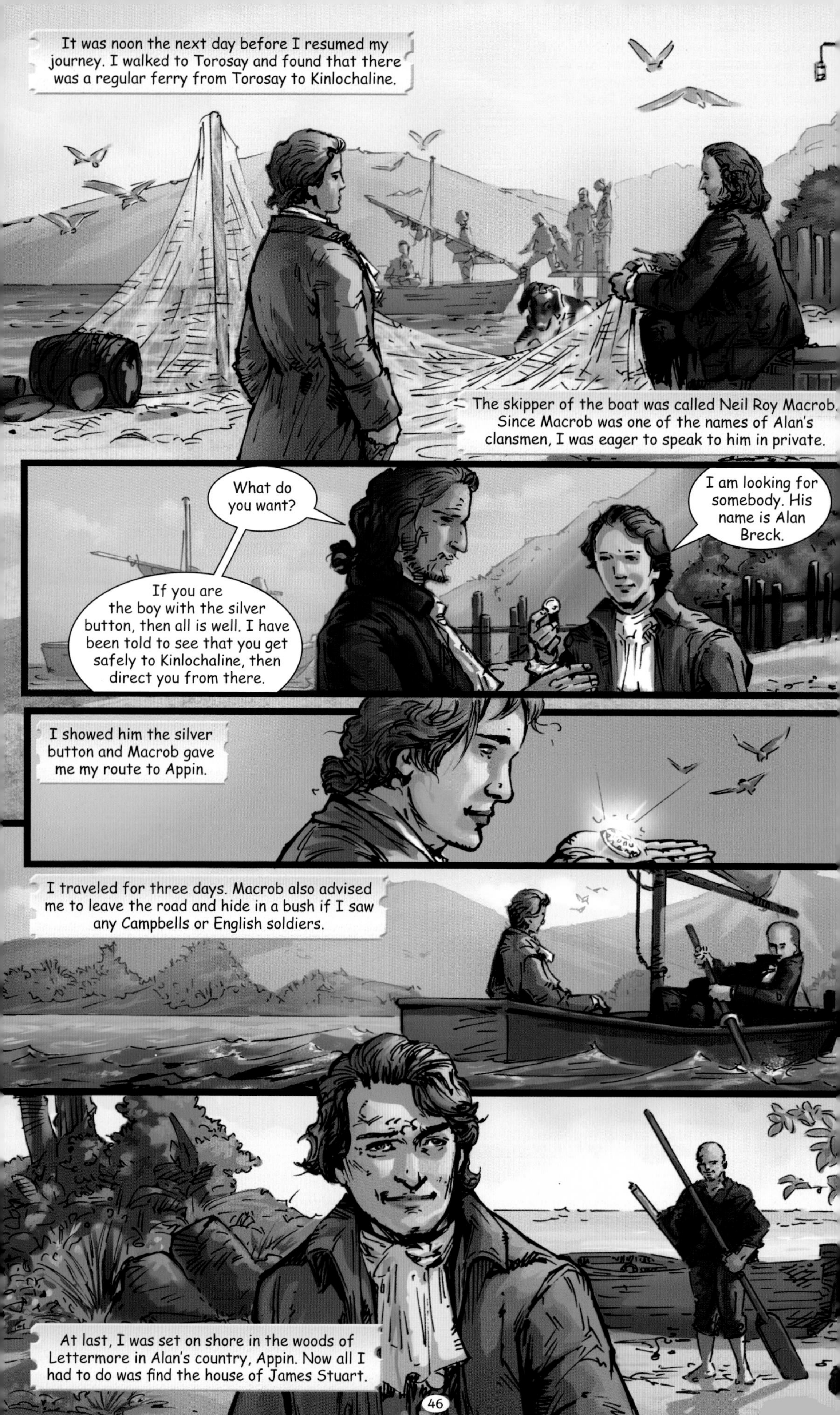

It was noon the next day before I resumed my journey. I walked to Torosay and found that there was a regular ferry from Torosay to Kinlochaline.
The skipper of the boat was called Neil Roy Macrob. Since Macrob was one of the names of Alan's clansmen, I was eager to speak to him in private.
What do you want?
I am looking for somebody. His name is Alan Breck.
If you are the boy with the silver button, then all is well. I have been told to see that you get safely to Kinlochaline, then direct you from there.
I showed him the silver button and Macrob gave me my route to Appin.
I traveled for three days. Macrob also advised me to leave the road and hide in a bush if I saw any Campbells or English soldiers.
At last, I was set on shore in the woods of Lettermore in Alan's country, Appin. Now all I had to do was find the house of James Stuart.

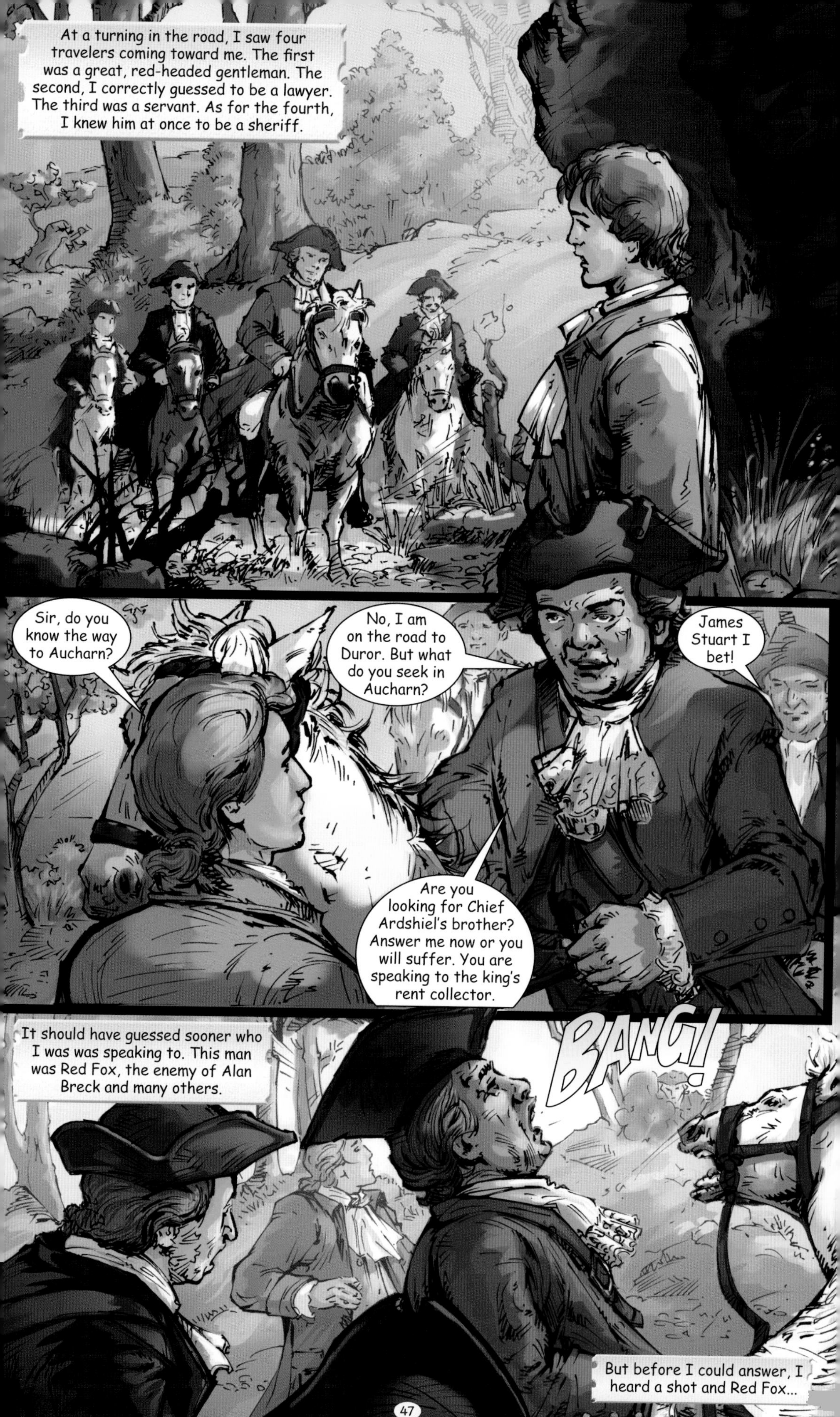

At a turning in the road, I saw four travelers coming toward me. The first was a great, red-headed gentleman. The second, I correctly guessed to be a lawyer. The third was a servant. As for the fourth, I knew him at once to be a sheriff.
Sir, do you know the way to Aucharn?
No, I am on the road to Duror. But what do you seek in Aucharn?
James Stuart I bet!
Are you looking for Chief Ardshiel's brother? Answer me now or you will suffer. You are speaking to the king's rent collector.
It should have guessed sooner who I was was speaking to. This man was Red Fox, the enemy of Alan Breck and many others.
BANG!
But before I could answer, I heard a shot and Red Fox...

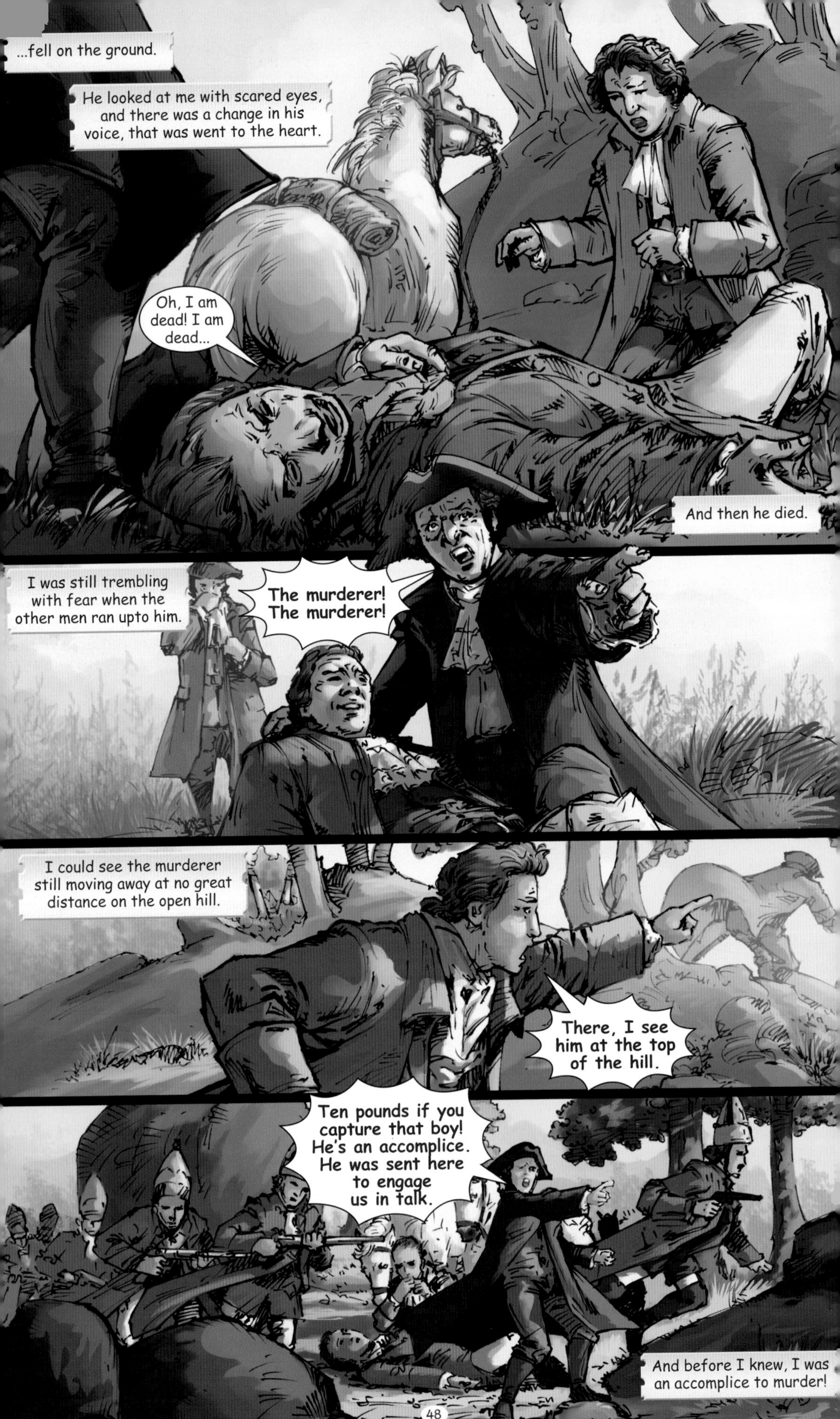
...fell on the ground.
He looked at me with scared eyes, and there was a change in his voice, that was went to the heart.
Oh, I am dead! I am dead...
And then he died.
I was still trembling with fear when the other men ran upto him.
The murderer! The murderer!
I could see the murderer still moving away at no great distance on the open hill.
There, I see him at the top of the hill.
Ten pounds if you capture that boy! He's an accomplice. He was sent here to engage us in talk.
And before I knew, I was an accomplice to murder!

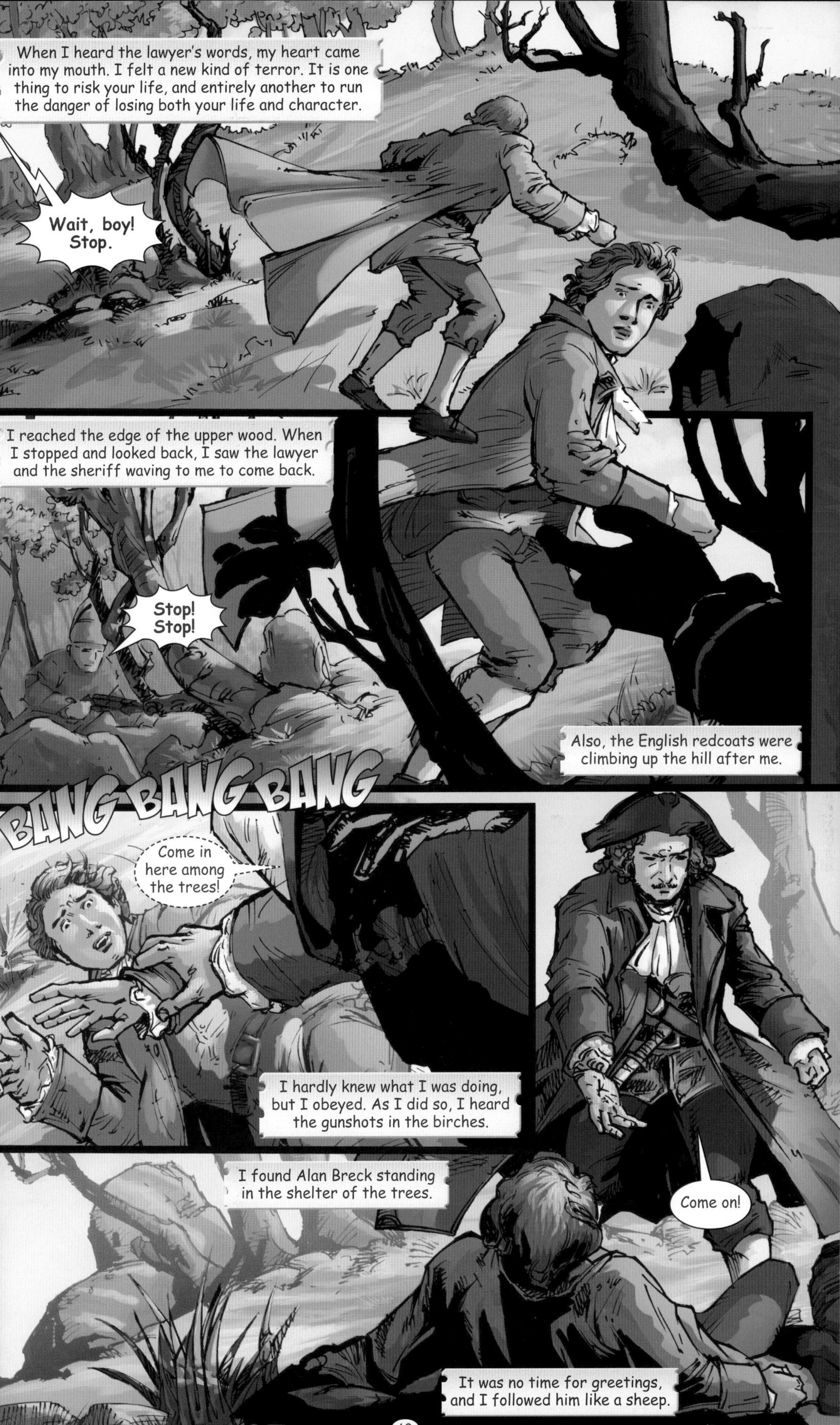
When I heard the lawyer's words, my heart came into my mouth. I felt a new kind of terror. It is one thing to risk your life, and entirely another to run the danger of losing both your life and character.
Wait, boy! Stop.
I reached the edge of the upper wood. When I stopped and looked back, I saw the lawyer and the sheriff waving to me to come back.
Stop! Stop!
Also, the English redcoats were climbing up the hill after me.
BANG BANG BANG
Come in here among the trees!
I hardly knew what I was doing, but I obeyed. As I did so, I heard the gunshots in the birches.
I found Alan Breck standing in the shelter of the trees.
Come on!
It was no time for greetings, and I followed him like a sheep.

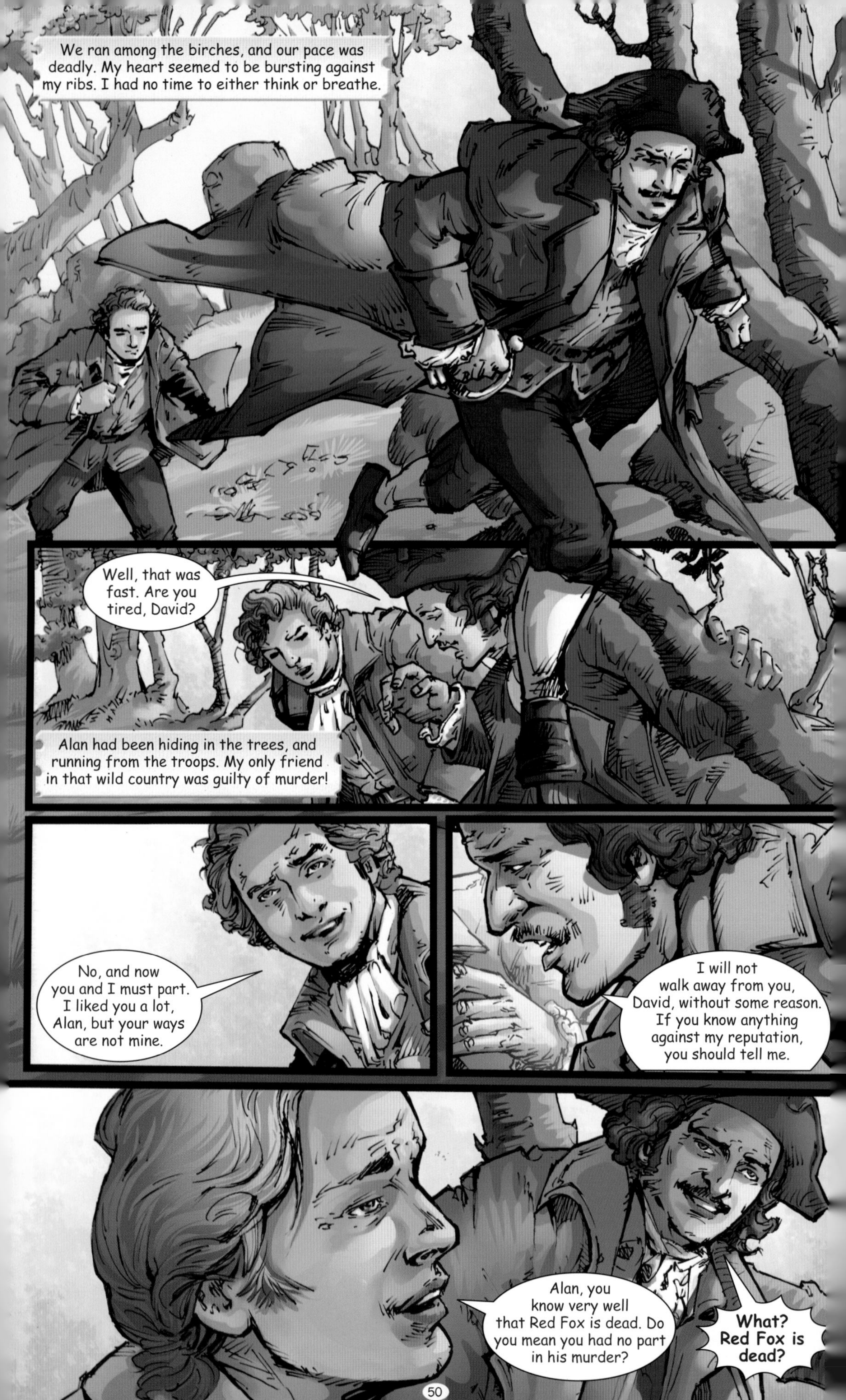
We ran among the birches, and our pace was deadly. My heart seemed to be bursting against my ribs. I had no time to either think or breathe.
Well, that was fast. Are you tired, David?
Alan had been hiding in the trees, and running from the troops. My only friend in that wild country was guilty of murder!
No, and now you and I must part. I liked you a lot, Alan, but your ways are not mine.
I will not walk away from you, David, without some reason. If you know anything against my reputation, you should tell me.
Alan, you know very well that Red Fox is dead. Do you mean you had no part in his murder?
What? Red Fox is dead?

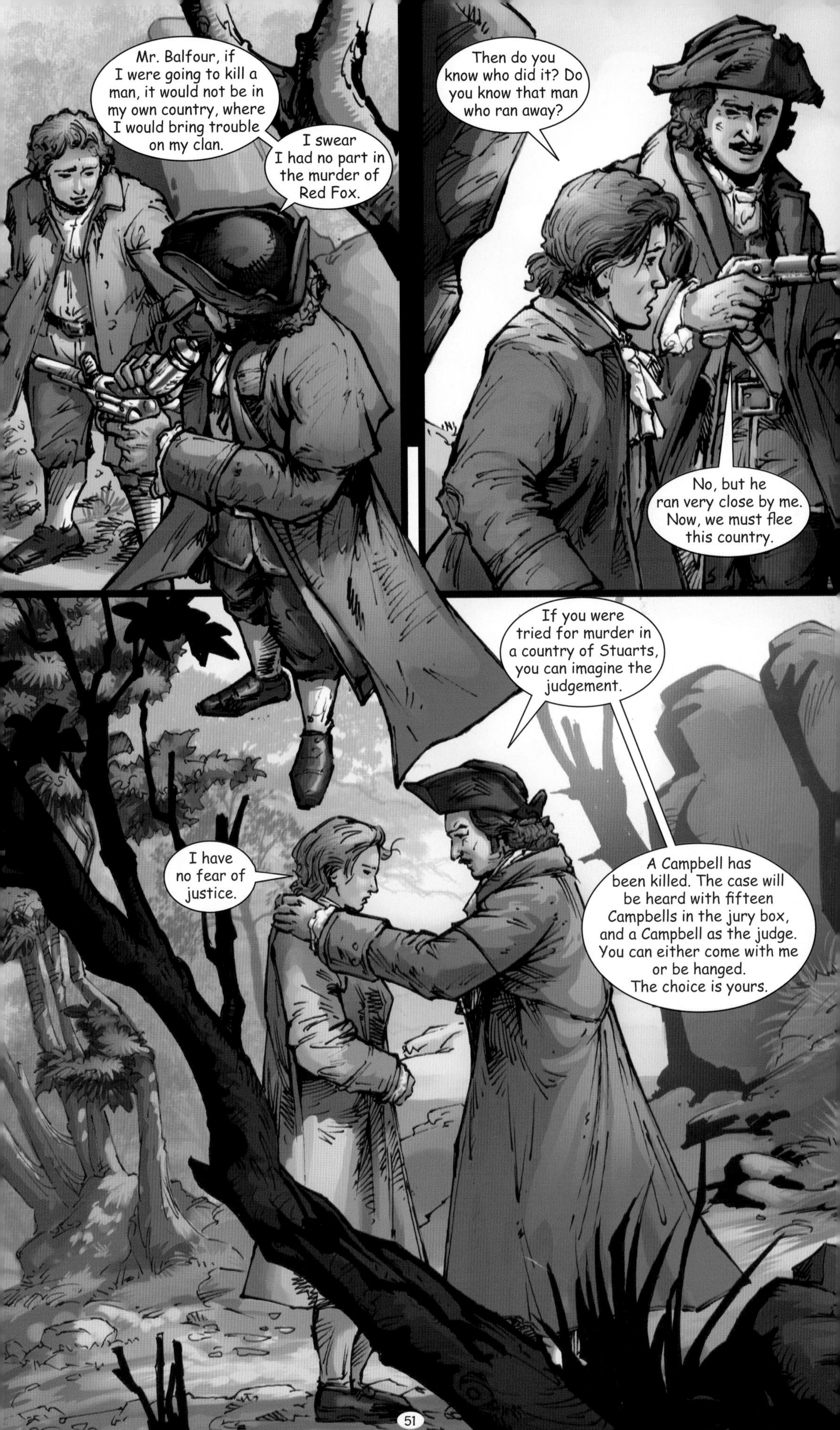

Mr. Balfour, if I were going to kill a man, it would not be in my own country, where I would bring trouble on my clan.
I swear I had no part in the murder of Red Fox.
Then do you know who did it? Do you know that man who ran away?
No, but he ran very close by me. Now, we must flee this country.
If you were tried for murder in a country of Stuarts, you can imagine the judgement.
I have no fear of justice.
A Campbell has been killed. The case will be heard with fifteen Campbells in the jury box, and a Campbell as the judge. You can either come with me or be hanged. The choice is yours.

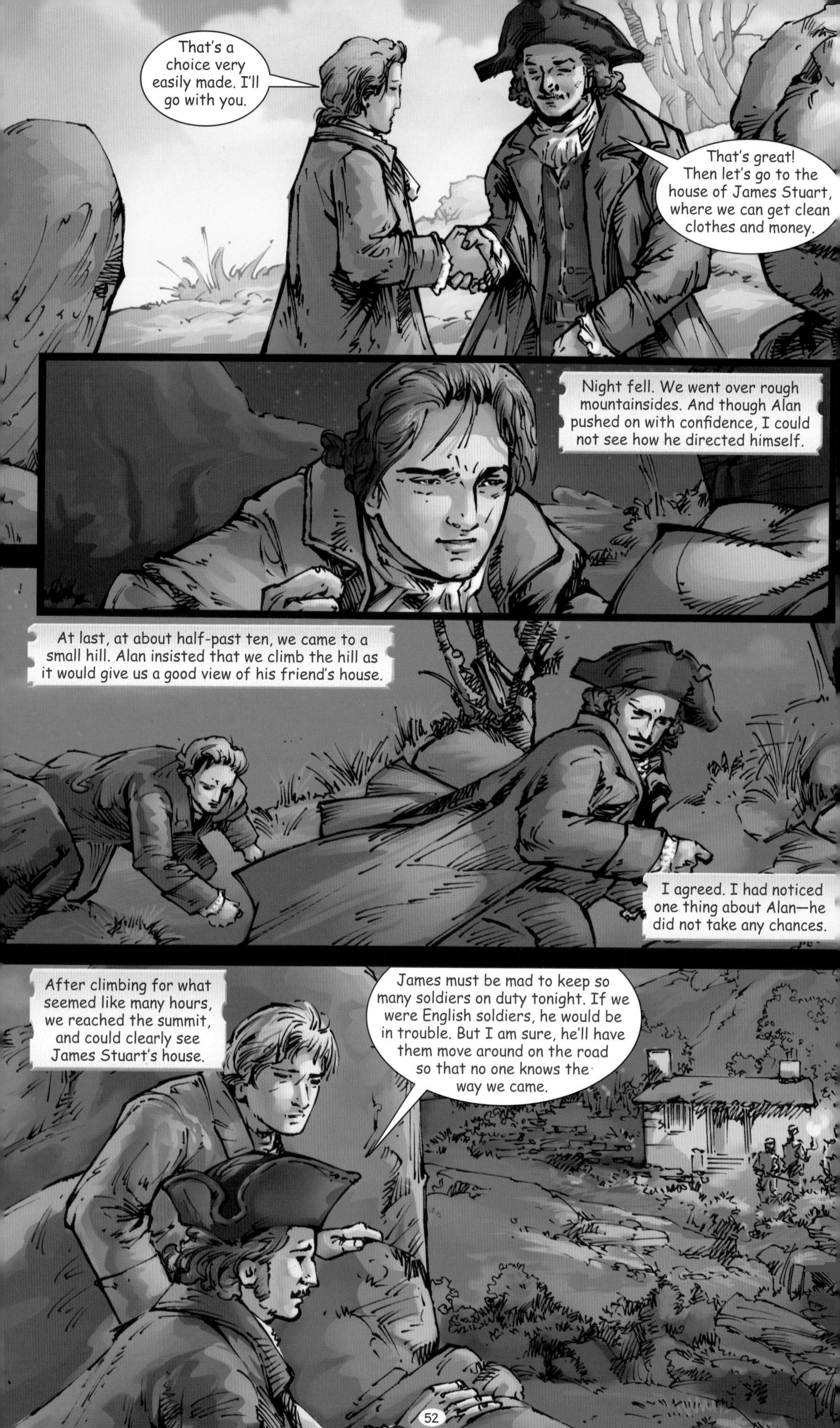
That's a choice very easily made. I'll go with you.
That's great! Then let's go to the house of James Stuart, where we can get clean clothes and money.
Night fell. We went over rough mountainsides. And though Alan pushed on with confidence, I could not see how he directed himself.
At last, at about half-past ten, we came to a small hill. Alan insisted that we climb the hill as it would give us a good view of his friend's house.
I agreed. I had noticed one thing about Alan—he did not take any chances.
After climbing for what seemed like many hours, we reached the summit, and could clearly see James Stuart's house.
James must be mad to keep so many soldiers on duty tonight. If we were English soldiers, he would be in trouble. But I am sure, he'll have them move around on the road so that no one knows the way we came.

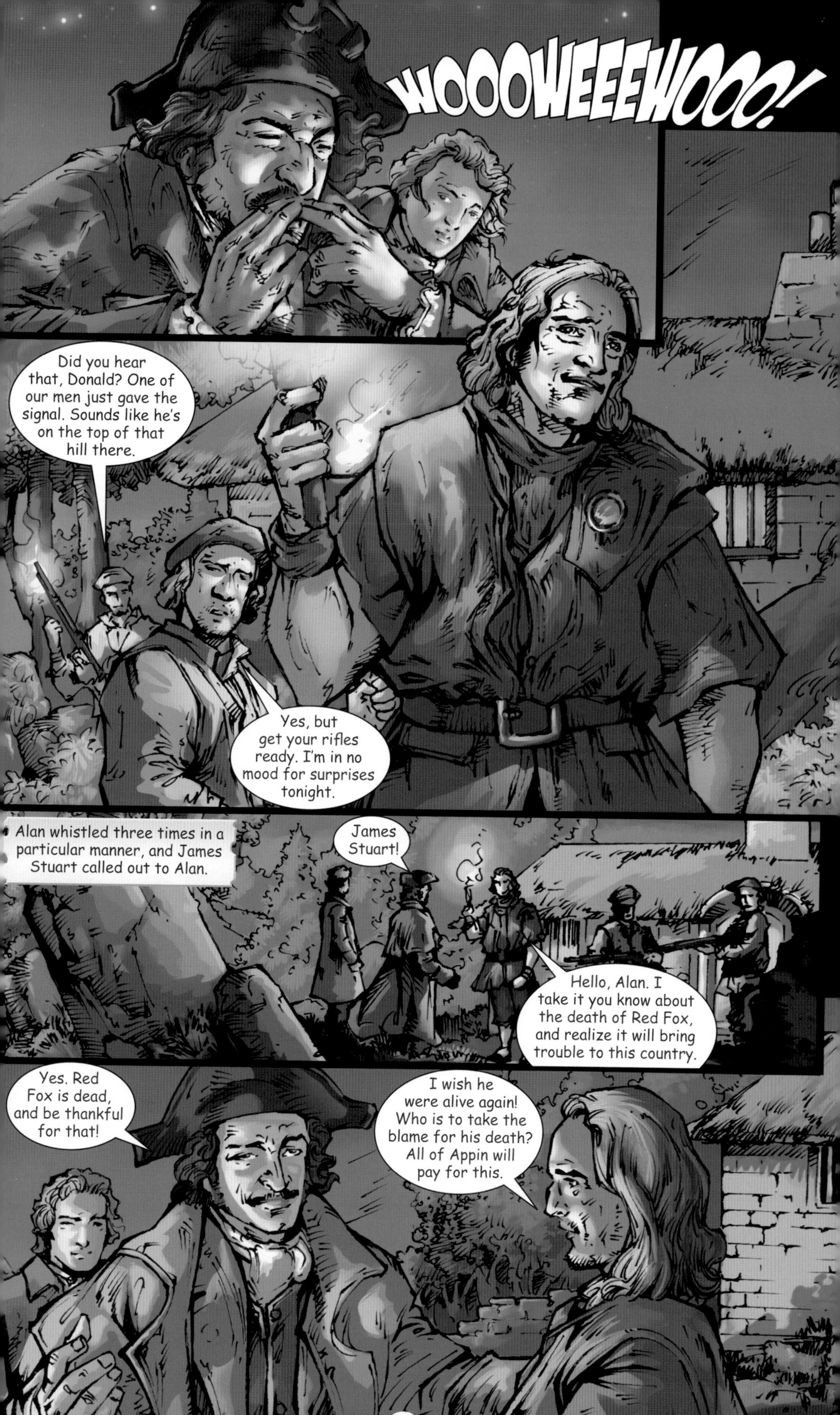
WOOOWEEEWOOO!
Did you hear that, Donald? One of our men just gave the signal. Sounds like he's on the top of that hill there.
Yes, but get your rifles ready. I'm in no mood for surprises tonight.
Alan whistled three times in a particular manner, and James Stuart called out to Alan.
James Stuart!
Hello, Alan. I take it you know about the death of Red Fox, and realize it will bring trouble to this country.
Yes. Red Fox is dead, and be thankful for that!
I wish he were alive again! Who is to take the blame for his death? All of Appin will pay for this.

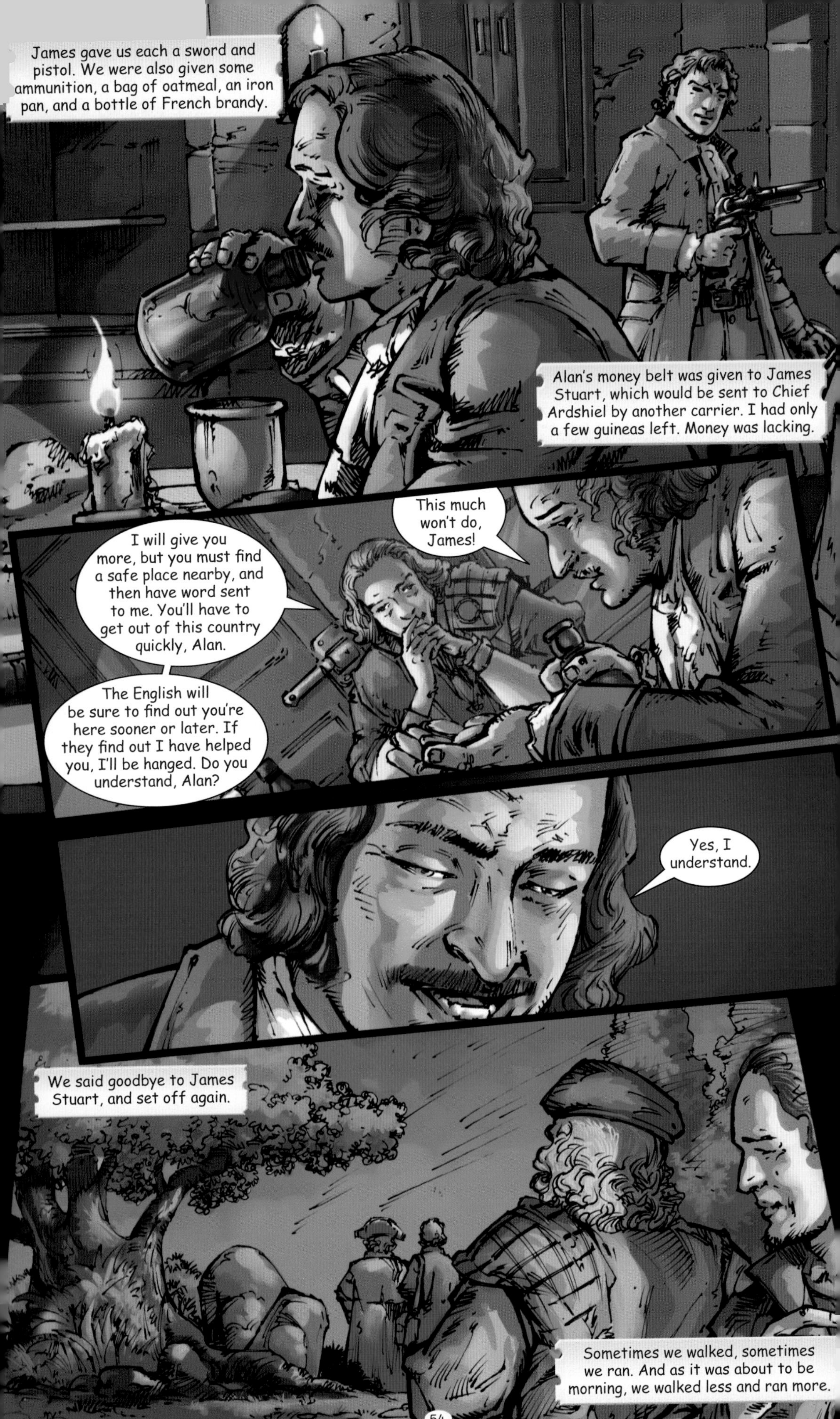

James gave us each a sword and pistol. We were also given some ammunition, a bag of oatmeal, an iron pan, and a bottle of French brandy.
Alan's money belt was given to James Stuart, which would be sent to Chief Ardshiel by another carrier. I had only a few guineas left. Money was lacking.
This much won't do, James!
I will give you more, but you must find a safe place nearby, and then have word sent to me. You'll have to get out of this country quickly, Alan.
The English will be sure to find out you're here sooner or later. If they find out I have helped you, I'll be hanged. Do you understand, Alan?
Yes, I understand.
We said goodbye to James Stuart, and set off again.
Sometimes we walked, sometimes we ran. And as it was about to be morning, we walked less and ran more.

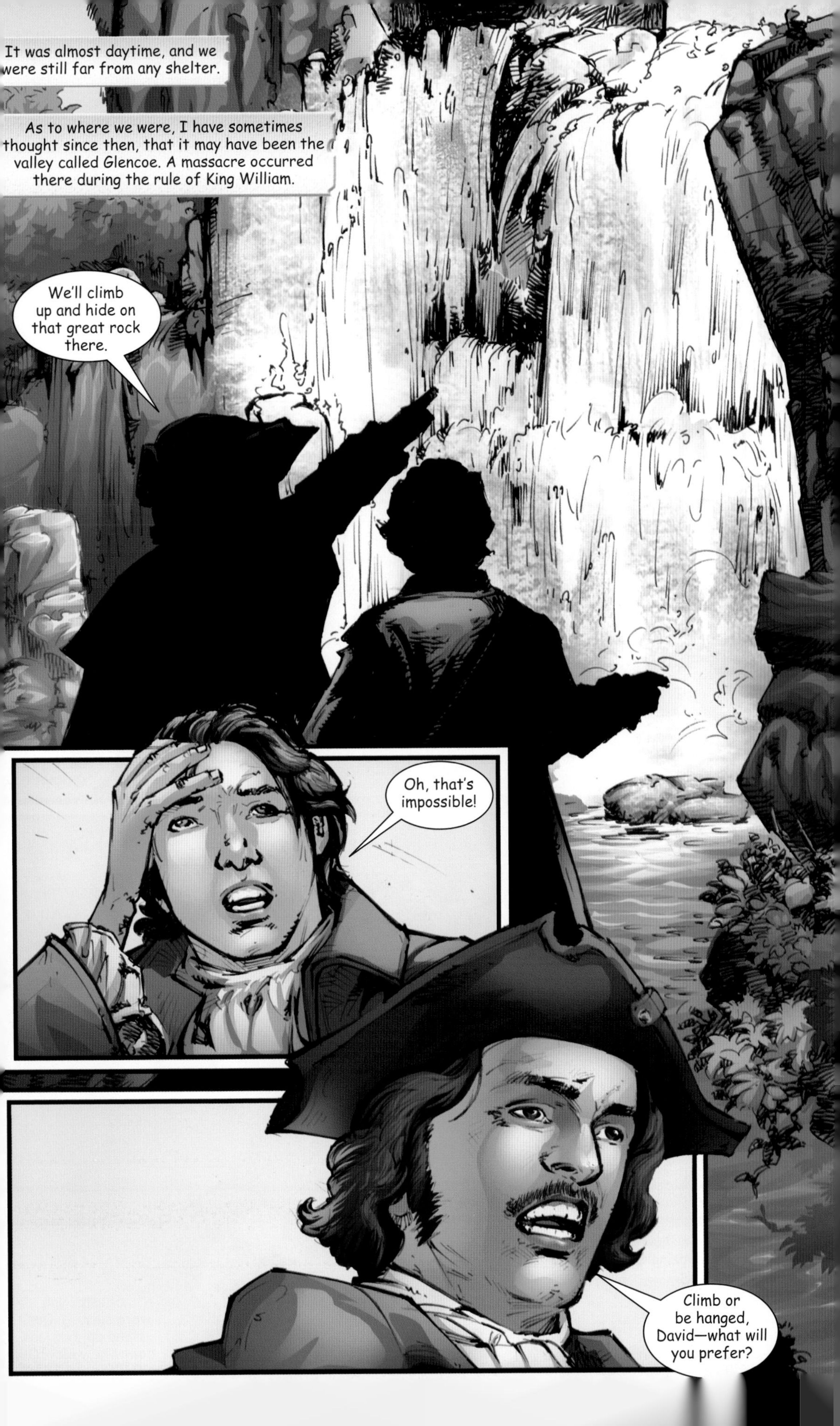

It was almost daytime, and we were still far from any shelter.
As to where we were, I have sometimes thought since then, that it may have been the valley called Glencoe. A massacre occurred there during the rule of King William.
We'll climb up and hide on that great rock there.
Oh, that's impossible!
Climb or be hanged, David—what will you prefer?

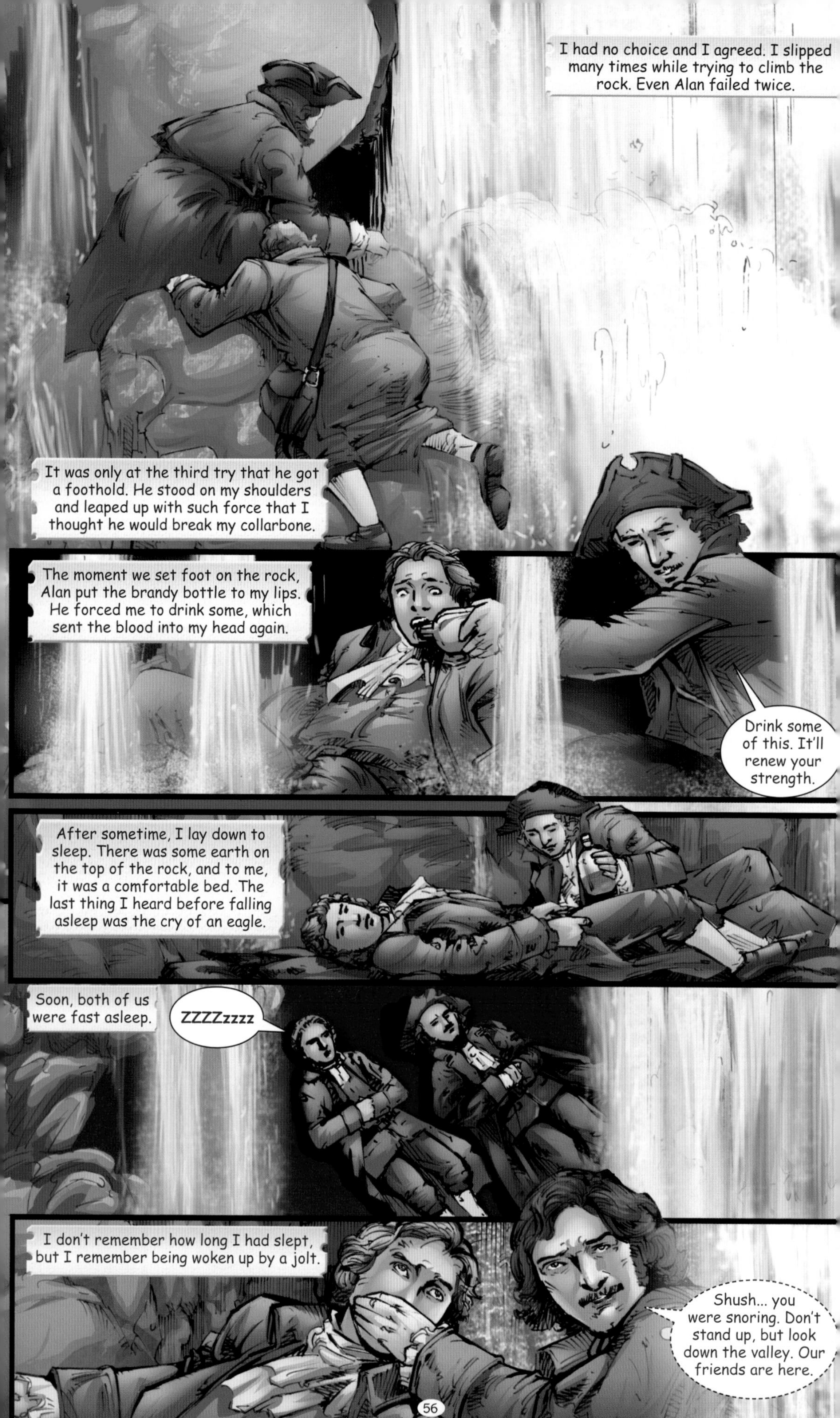

I had no choice and I agreed. I slipped many times while trying to climb the rock. Even Alan failed twice.
It was only at the third try that he got a foothold. He stood on my shoulders and leaped up with such force that I thought he would break my collarbone.
The moment we set foot on the rock, Alan put the brandy bottle to my lips. He forced me to drink some, which sent the blood into my head again.
Drink some of this. It'll renew your strength.
After sometime, I lay down to sleep. There was some earth on the top of the rock, and to me, it was a comfortable bed. The last thing I heard before falling asleep was the cry of an eagle.
Soon, both of us were fast asleep.
ZZZZzzzz
I don't remember how long I had slept, but I remember being woken up by a jolt.
Shush... you were snoring. Don't stand up, but look down the valley. Our friends are here.

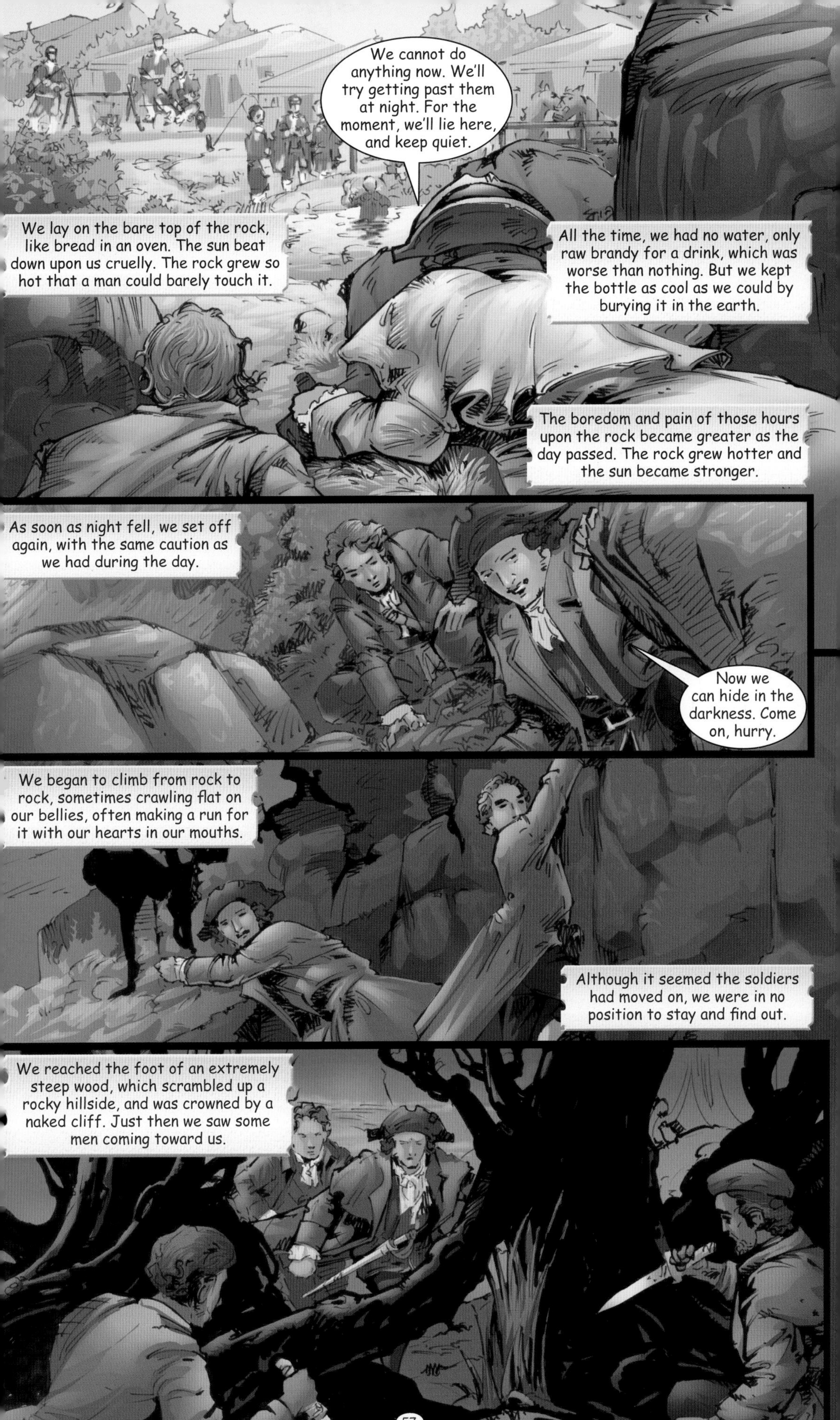
We cannot do anything now. We'll try getting past them at night. For the moment, we'll lie here, and keep quiet.
We lay on the bare top of the rock, like bread in an oven. The sun beat down upon us cruelly. The rock grew so hot that a man could barely touch it.
All the time, we had no water, only raw brandy for a drink, which was worse than nothing. But we kept the bottle as cool as we could by burying it in the earth.
The boredom and pain of those hours upon the rock became greater as the day passed. The rock grew hotter and the sun became stronger.
As soon as night fell, we set off again, with the same caution as we had during the day.
Now we can hide in the darkness. Come on, hurry.
We began to climb from rock to rock, sometimes crawling flat on our bellies, often making a run for it with our hearts in our mouths.
Although it seemed the soldiers had moved on, we were in no position to stay and find out.
We reached the foot of an extremely steep wood, which scrambled up a rocky hillside, and was crowned by a naked cliff. Just then we saw some men coming toward us.

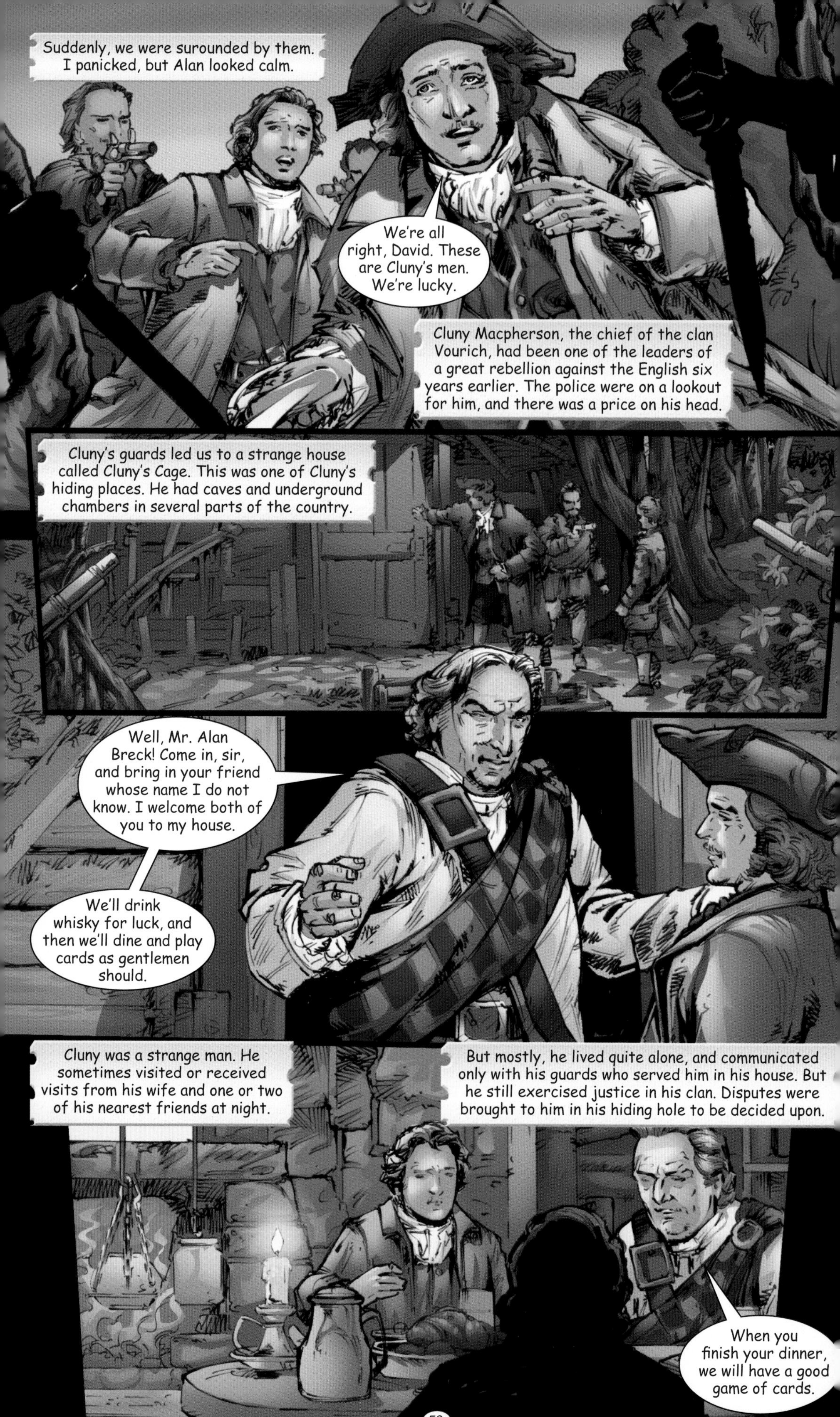
Suddenly, we were surounded by them. I panicked, but Alan looked calm.
We're all right, David. These are Cluny's men. We're lucky.
Cluny Macpherson, the chief of the clan Vourich, had been one of the leaders of a great rebellion against the English six years earlier. The police were on a lookout for him, and there was a price on his head.
Cluny's guards led us to a strange house called Cluny's Cage. This was one of Cluny's hiding places. He had caves and underground chambers in several parts of the country.
Well, Mr. Alan Breck! Come in, sir, and bring in your friend whose name I do not know. I welcome both of you to my house.
We'll drink whisky for luck, and then we'll dine and play cards as gentlemen should.
Cluny was a strange man. He sometimes visited or received visits from his wife and one or two of his nearest friends at night.
But mostly, he lived quite alone, and communicated only with his guards who served him in his house. But he still exercised justice in his clan. Disputes were brought to him in his hiding hole to be decided upon.
When you finish your dinner, we will have a good game of cards.

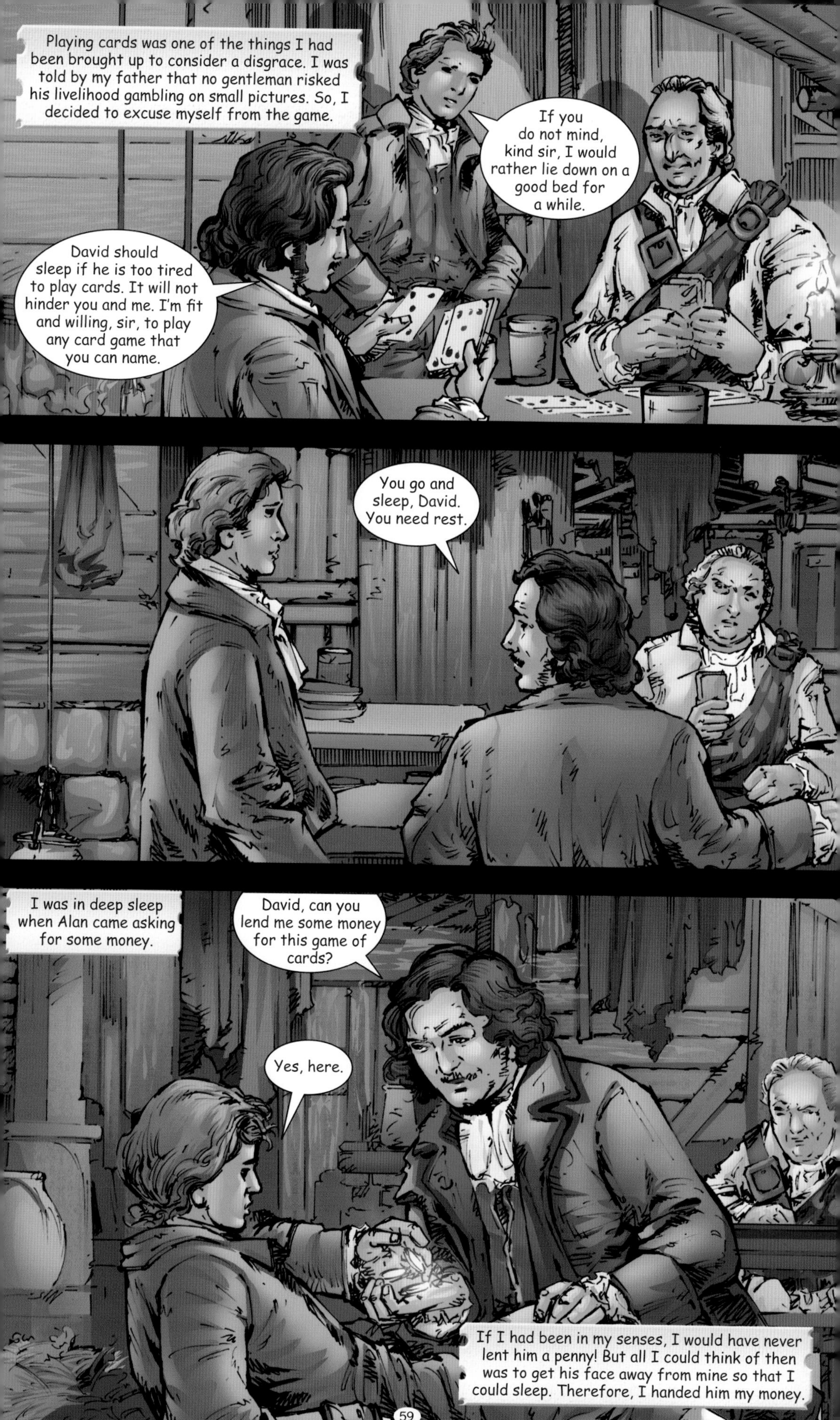

Playing cards was one of the things I had been brought up to consider a disgrace. I was told by my father that no gentleman risked his livelihood gambling on small pictures. So, I decided to excuse myself from the game.
If you do not mind, kind sir, I would rather lie down on a good bed for a while.
David should sleep if he is too tired to play cards. It will not hinder you and me. I'm fit and willing, sir, to play any card game that you can name.
You go and sleep, David. You need rest.
I was in deep sleep when Alan came asking for some money.
David, can you lend me some money for this game of cards?
Yes, here.
If I had been in my senses, I would have never lent him a penny! But all I could think of then was to get his face away from mine so that I could sleep. Therefore, I handed him my money.

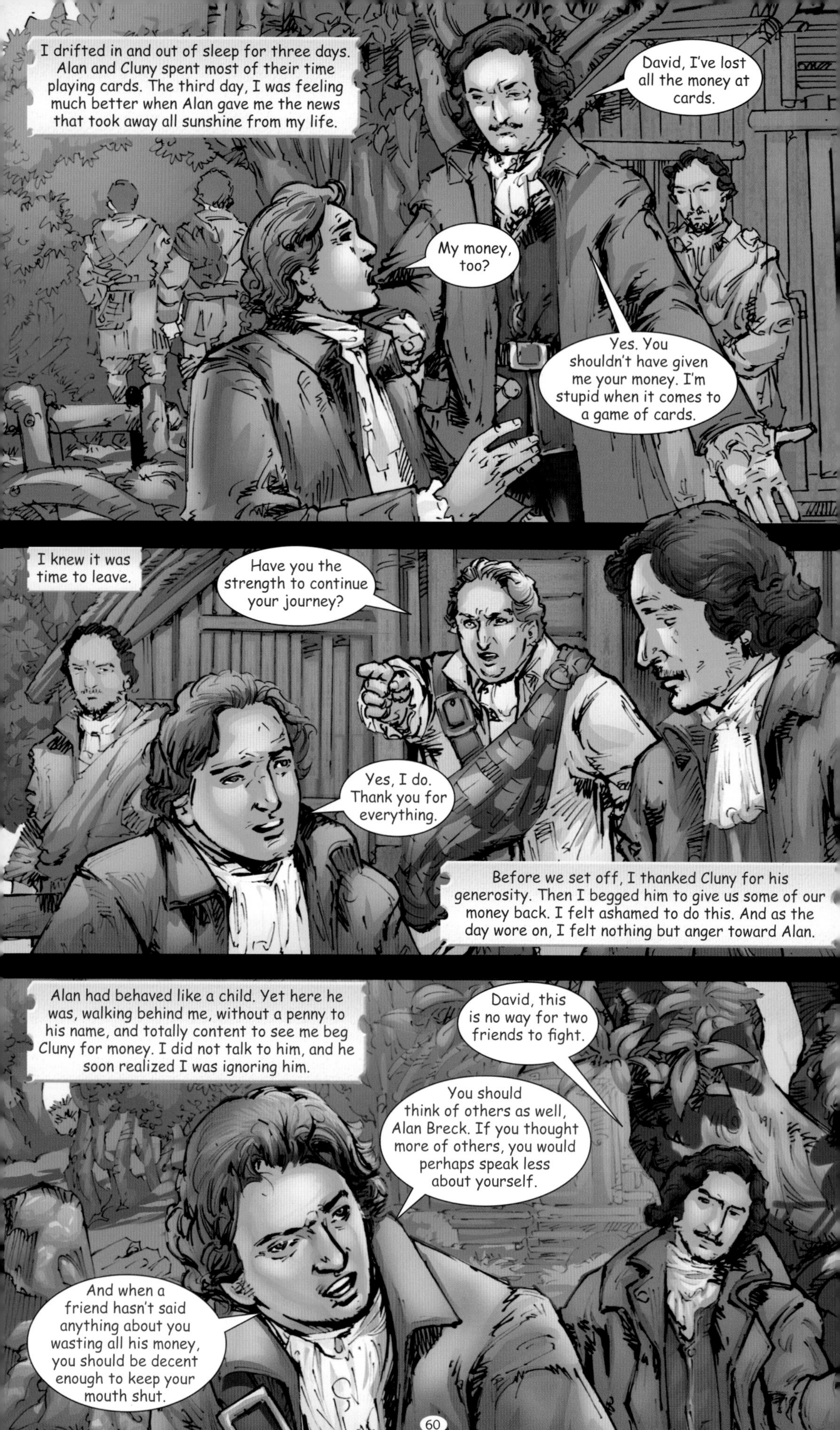
I drifted in and out of sleep for three days. Alan and Cluny spent most of their time playing cards. The third day, I was feeling much better when Alan gave me the news that took away all sunshine from my life.
David, I've lost all the money at cards.
My money, too?
Yes. You shouldn't have given me your money. I'm stupid when it comes to a game of cards.
I knew it was time to leave.
Have you the strength to continue your journey?
Yes, I do. Thank you for everything.
Before we set off, I thanked Cluny for his generosity. Then I begged him to give us some of our money back. I felt ashamed to do this. And as the day wore on, I felt nothing but anger toward Alan.
Alan had behaved like a child. Yet here he was, walking behind me, without a penny to his name, and totally content to see me beg Cluny for money. I did not talk to him, and he soon realized I was ignoring him.
David, this is no way for two friends to fight.
You should think of others as well, Alan Breck. If you thought more of others, you would perhaps speak less about yourself.
And when a friend hasn't said anything about you wasting all his money, you should be decent enough to keep your mouth shut.

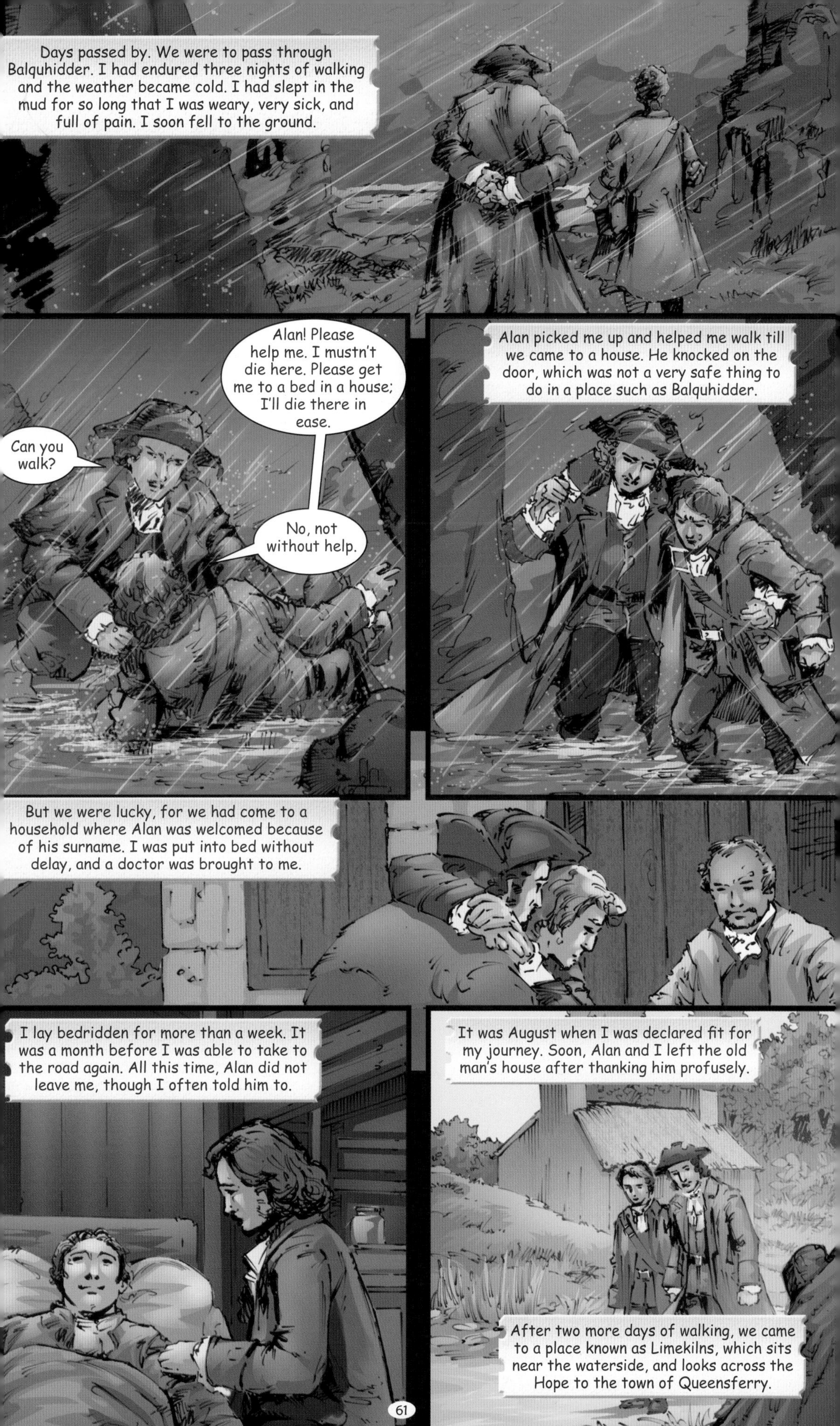
Days passed by. We were to pass through Balquhidder. I had endured three nights of walking and the weather became cold. I had slept in the mud for so long that I was weary, very sick, and full of pain. I soon fell to the ground.
Can you walk?
Alan! Please help me. I mustn't die here. Please get me to a bed in a house; I'll die there in ease.
No, not without help.
Alan picked me up and helped me walk till we came to a house. He knocked on the door, which was not a very safe thing to do in a place such as Balquhidder.
But we were lucky, for we had come to a household where Alan was welcomed because of his surname. I was put into bed without delay, and a doctor was brought to me.
I lay bedridden for more than a week. It was a month before I was able to take to the road again. All this time, Alan did not leave me, though I often told him to.
It was August when I was declared fit for my journey. Soon, Alan and I left the old man's house after thanking him profusely.
After two more days of walking, we came to a place known as Limekilns, which sits near the waterside, and looks across the Hope to the town of Queensferry.

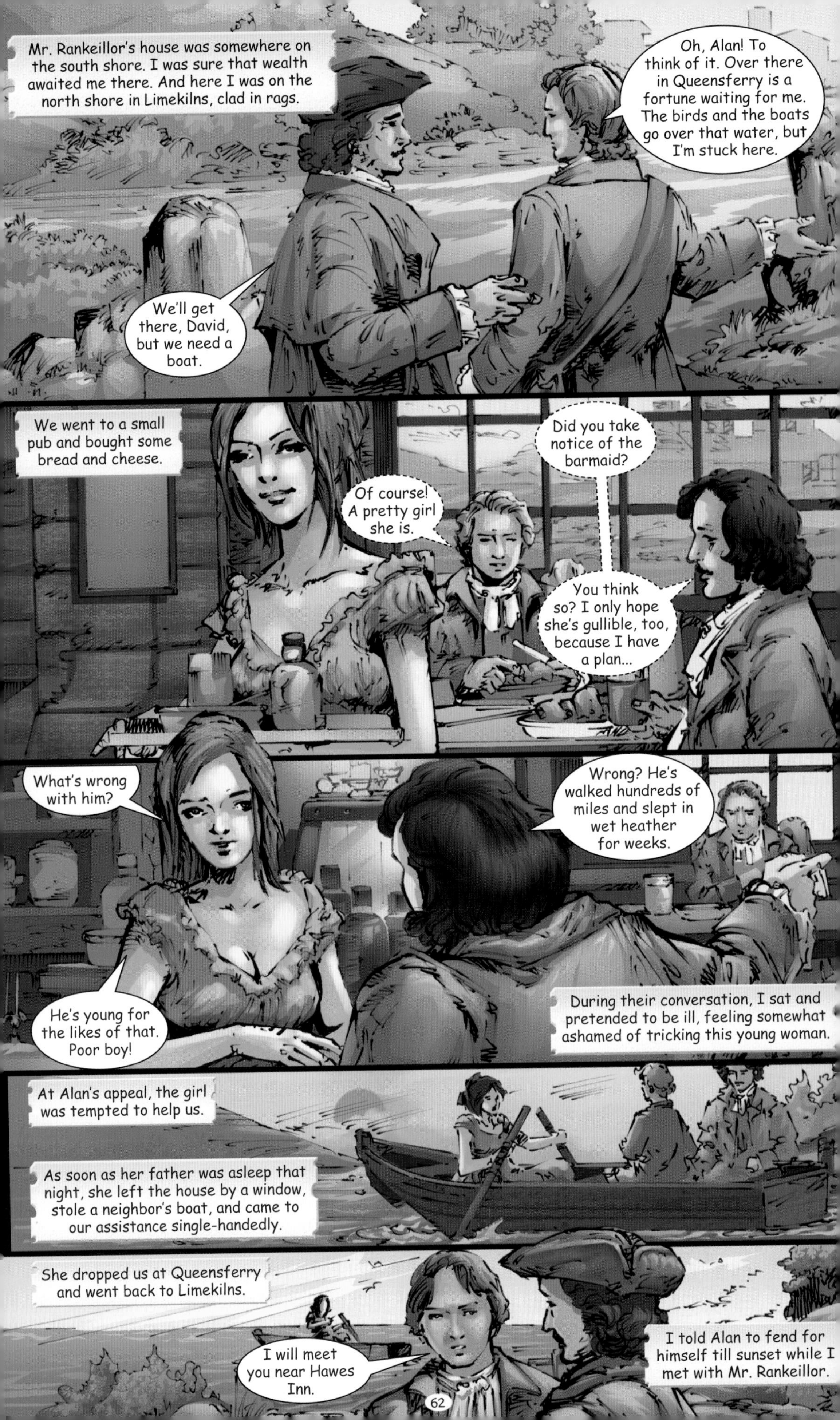
Mr. Rankeillor's house was somewhere on the south shore. I was sure that wealth awaited me there. And here I was on the north shore in Limekilns, clad in rags.
Oh, Alan! To think of it. Over there in Queensferry is a fortune waiting for me. The birds and the boats go over that water, but I'm stuck here.
We'll get there, David, but we need a boat.
We went to a small pub and bought some bread and cheese.
Did you take notice of the barmaid?
Of course! A pretty girl she is.
You think so? I only hope she's gullible, too, because I have a plan...
What's wrong with him?
Wrong? He's walked hundreds of miles and slept in wet heather for weeks.
He's young for the likes of that. Poor boy!
During their conversation, I sat and pretended to be ill, feeling somewhat ashamed of tricking this young woman.
At Alan's appeal, the girl was tempted to help us.
As soon as her father was asleep that night, she left the house by a window, stole a neighbor's boat, and came to our assistance single-handedly.
She dropped us at Queensferry and went back to Limekilns.
I will meet you near Hawes Inn.
I told Alan to fend for himself till sunset while I met with Mr. Rankeillor.

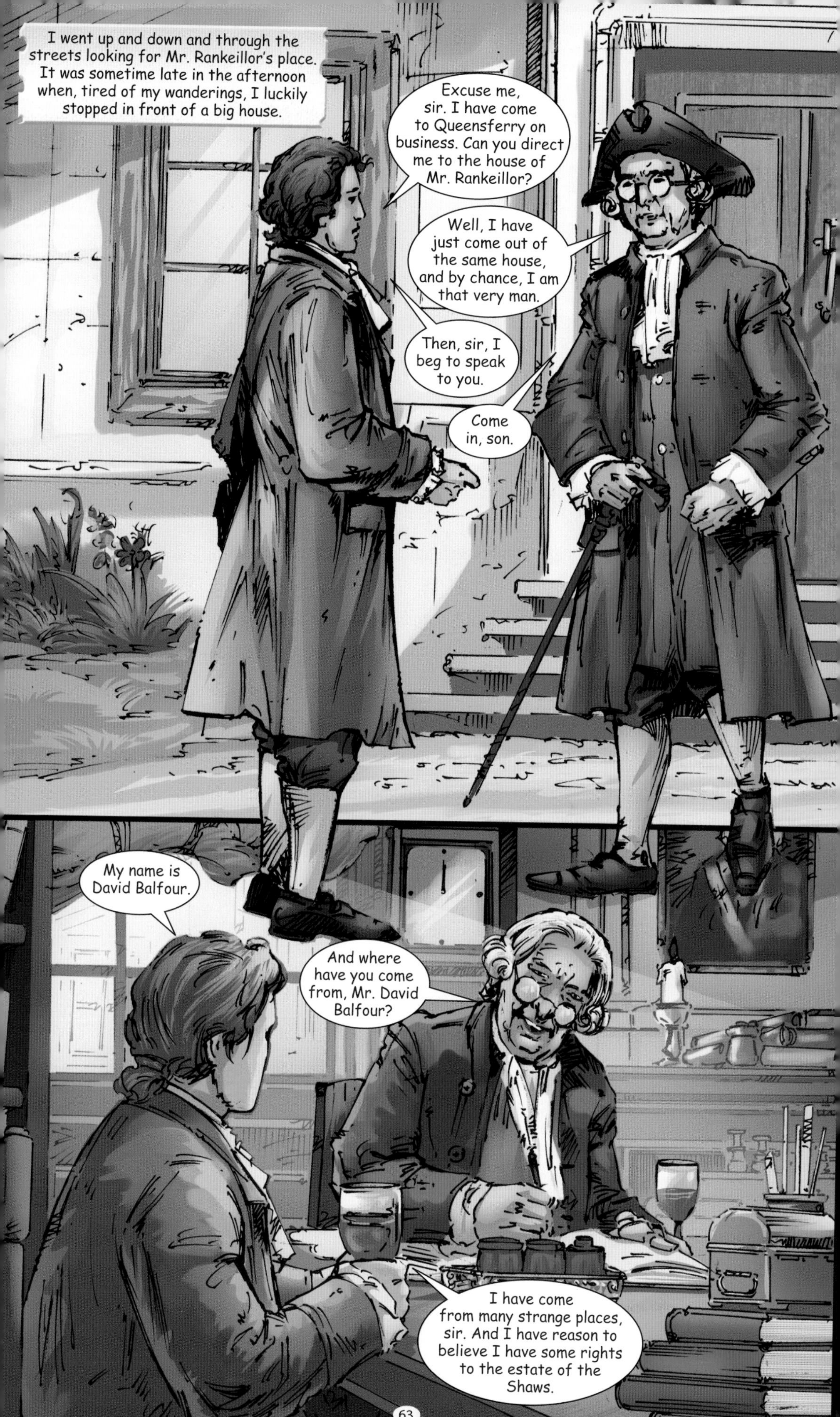
I went up and down and through the streets looking for Mr. Rankeillor's place. It was sometime late in the afternoon when, tired of my wanderings, I luckily stopped in front of a big house.
Excuse me, sir. I have come to Queensferry on business. Can you direct me to the house of Mr. Rankeillor?
Well, I have just come out of the same house, and by chance, I am that very man.
Then, sir, I beg to speak to you.
Come in, son.
My name is David Balfour.
And where have you come from, Mr. David Balfour?
I have come from many strange places, sir. And I have reason to believe I have some rights to the estate of the Shaws.

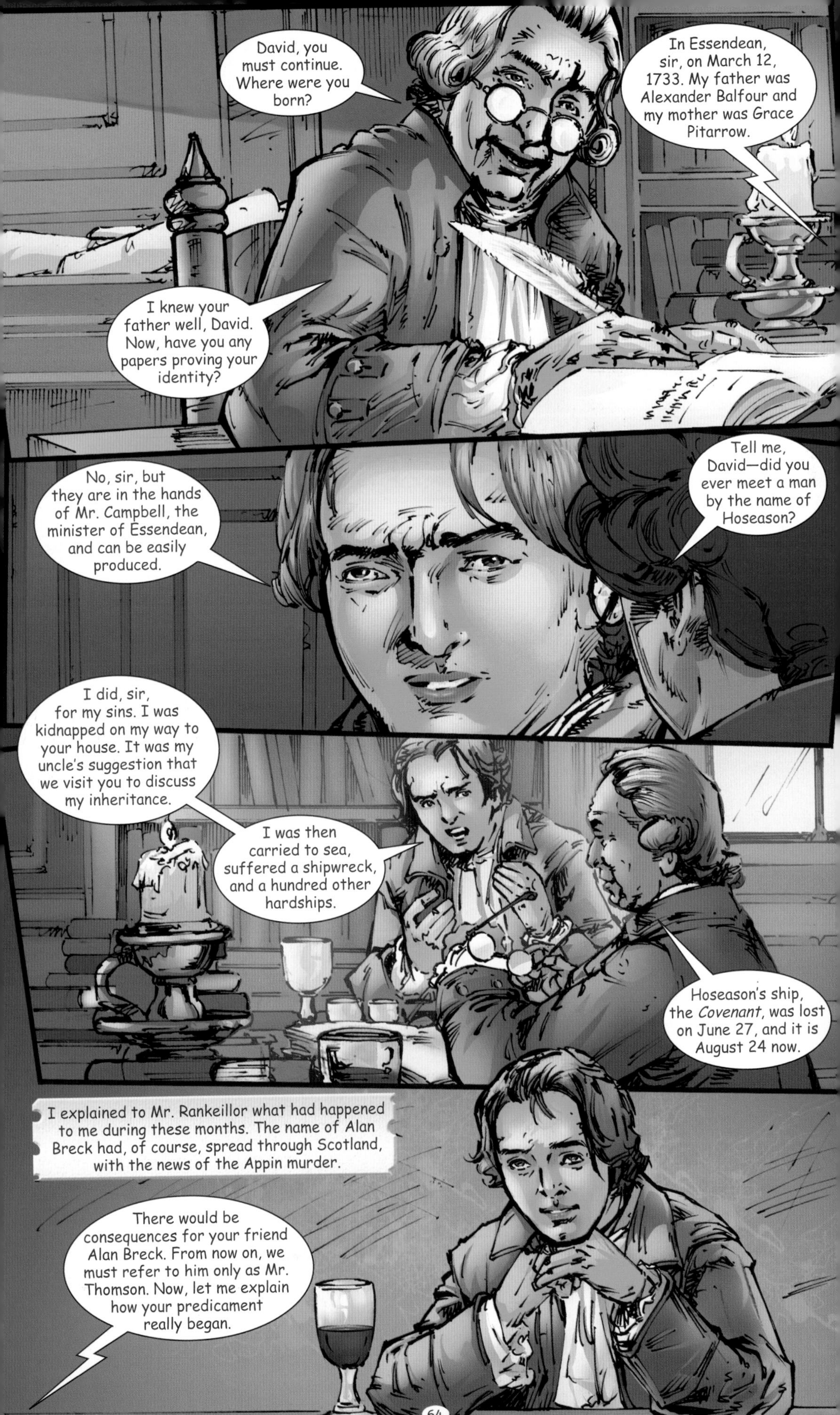
David, you must continue. Where were you born?
In Essendean, sir, on March 12, 1733. My father was Alexander Balfour and my mother was Grace Pitarrow.
I knew your father well, David. Now, have you any papers proving your identity?
No, sir, but they are in the hands of Mr. Campbell, the minister of Essendean, and can be easily produced.
Tell me, David—did you ever meet a man by the name of Hoseason?
I did, sir, for my sins. I was kidnapped on my way to your house. It was my uncle's suggestion that we visit you to discuss my inheritance.
I was then carried to sea, suffered a shipwreck, and a hundred other hardships.
Hoseason's ship, the *Covenant*, was lost on June 27, and it is August 24 now.
I explained to Mr. Rankeillor what had happened to me during these months. The name of Alan Breck had, of course, spread through Scotland, with the news of the Appin murder.
There would be consequences for your friend Alan Breck. From now on, we must refer to him only as Mr. Thomson. Now, let me explain how your predicament really began.

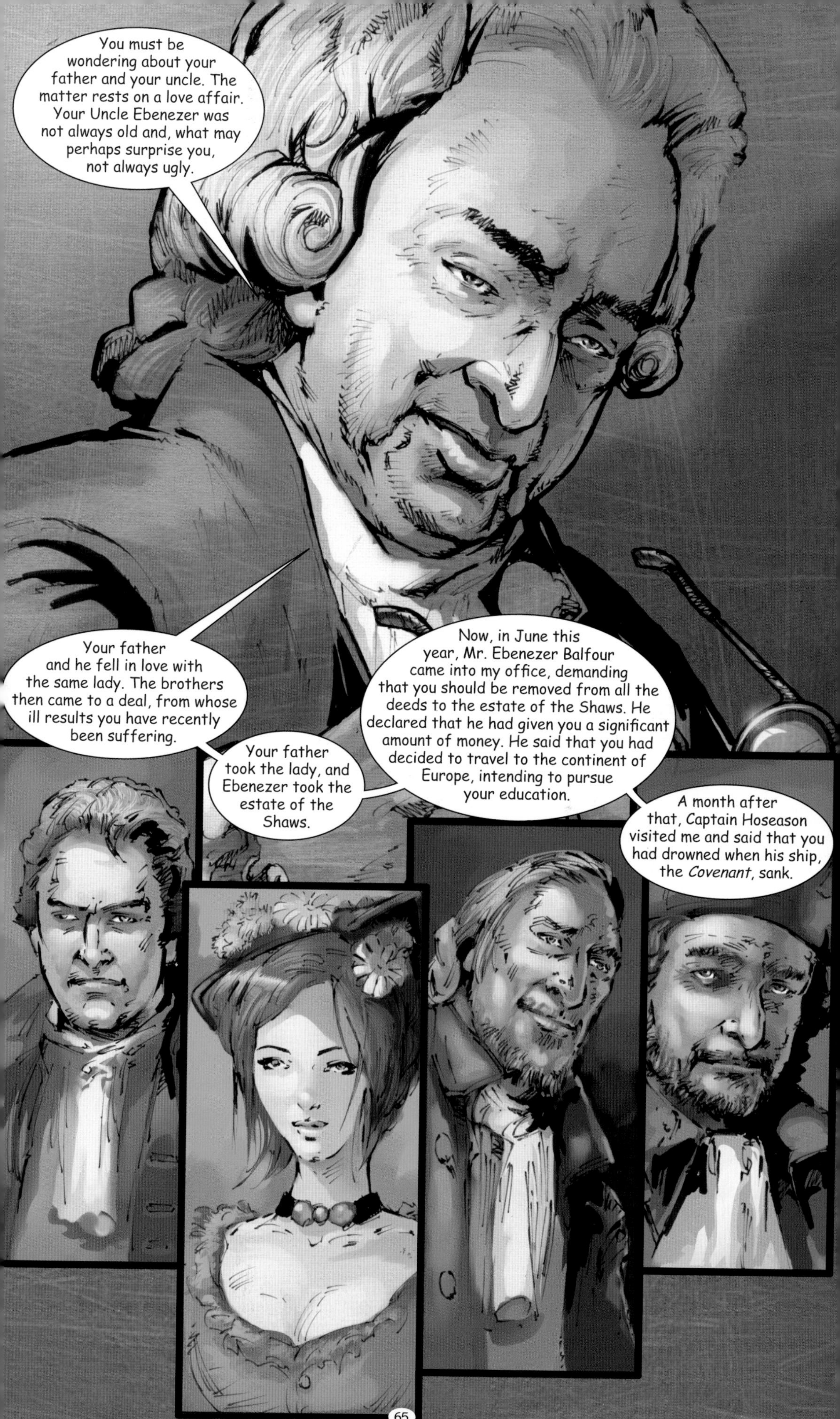
You must be wondering about your father and your uncle. The matter rests on a love affair. Your Uncle Ebenezer was not always old and, what may perhaps surprise you, not always ugly.
Your father and he fell in love with the same lady. The brothers then came to a deal, from whose ill results you have recently been suffering.
Your father took the lady, and Ebenezer took the estate of the Shaws.
Now, in June this year, Mr. Ebenezer Balfour came into my office, demanding that you should be removed from all the deeds to the estate of the Shaws. He declared that he had given you a significant amount of money. He said that you had decided to travel to the continent of Europe, intending to pursue your education.
A month after that, Captain Hoseason visited me and said that you had drowned when his ship, the *Covenant*, sank.

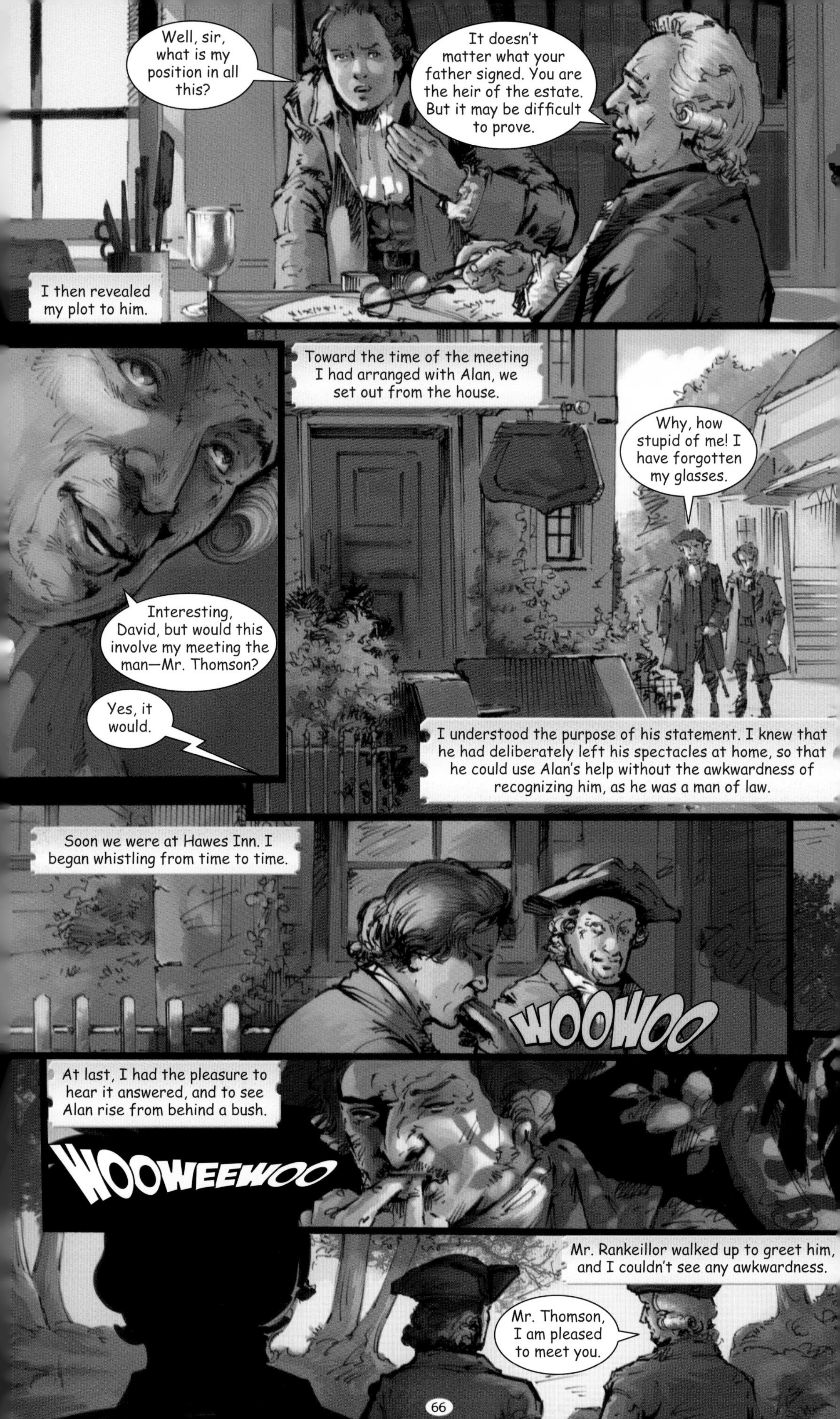
Well, sir, what is my position in all this?
It doesn't matter what your father signed. You are the heir of the estate. But it may be difficult to prove.
I then revealed my plot to him.
Interesting, David, but would this involve my meeting the man—Mr. Thomson?
Yes, it would.
Toward the time of the meeting I had arranged with Alan, we set out from the house.
Why, how stupid of me! I have forgotten my glasses.
I understood the purpose of his statement. I knew that he had deliberately left his spectacles at home, so that he could use Alan's help without the awkwardness of recognizing him, as he was a man of law.
Soon we were at Hawes Inn. I began whistling from time to time.
WOOWOO
At last, I had the pleasure to hear it answered, and to see Alan rise from behind a bush.
WOOWEEWOO
Mr. Rankeillor walked up to greet him, and I couldn't see any awkwardness.
Mr. Thomson, I am pleased to meet you.

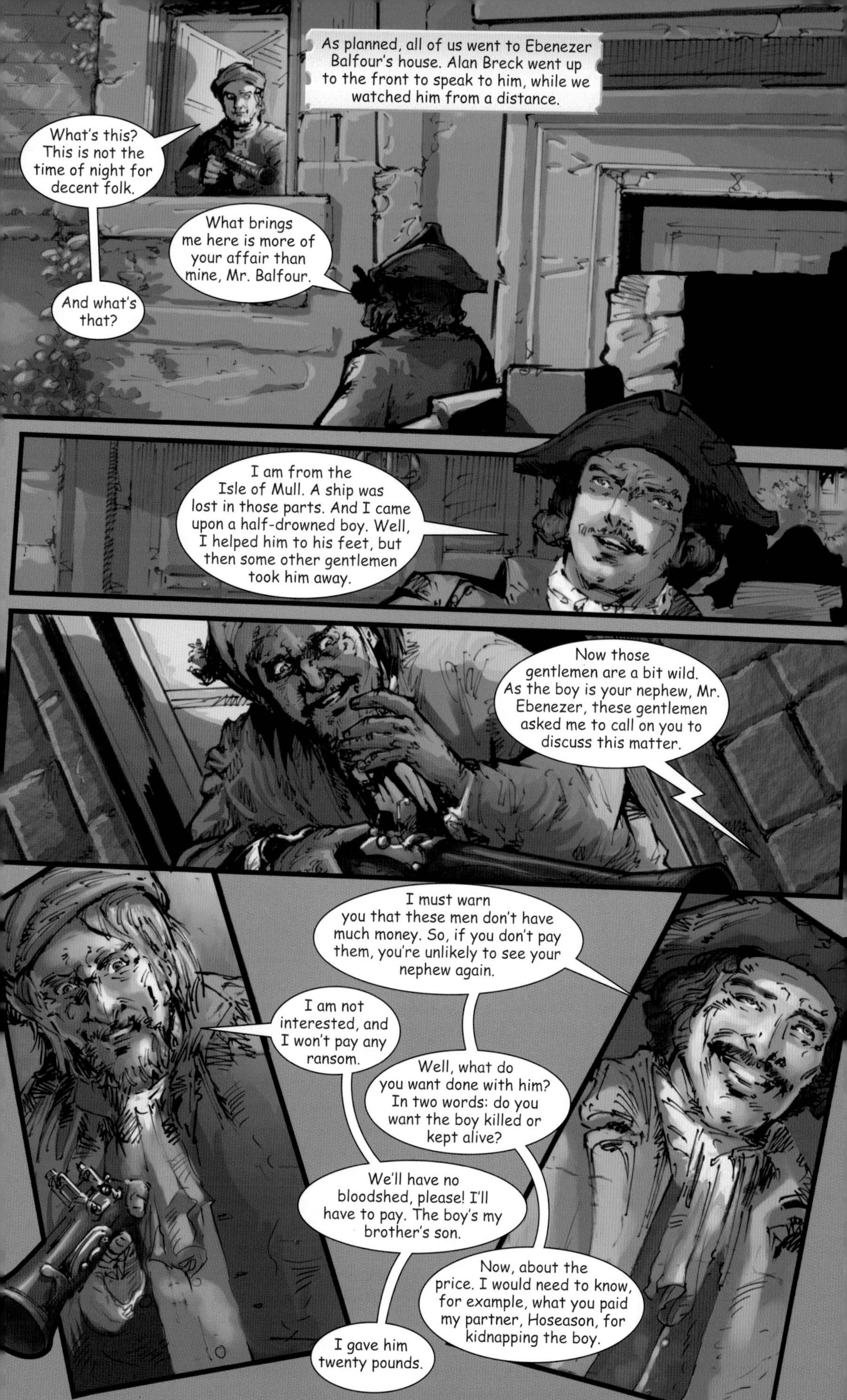

As planned, all of us went to Ebenezer Balfour's house. Alan Breck went up to the front to speak to him, while we watched him from a distance.
What's this? This is not the time of night for decent folk.
What brings me here is more of your affair than mine, Mr. Balfour.
And what's that?
I am from the Isle of Mull. A ship was lost in those parts. And I came upon a half-drowned boy. Well, I helped him to his feet, but then some other gentlemen took him away.
Now those gentlemen are a bit wild. As the boy is your nephew, Mr. Ebenezer, these gentlemen asked me to call on you to discuss this matter.
I must warn you that these men don't have much money. So, if you don't pay them, you're unlikely to see your nephew again.
I am not interested, and I won't pay any ransom.
Well, what do you want done with him? In two words: do you want the boy killed or kept alive?
We'll have no bloodshed, please! I'll have to pay. The boy's my brother's son.
Now, about the price. I would need to know, for example, what you paid my partner, Hoseason, for kidnapping the boy.
I gave him twenty pounds.

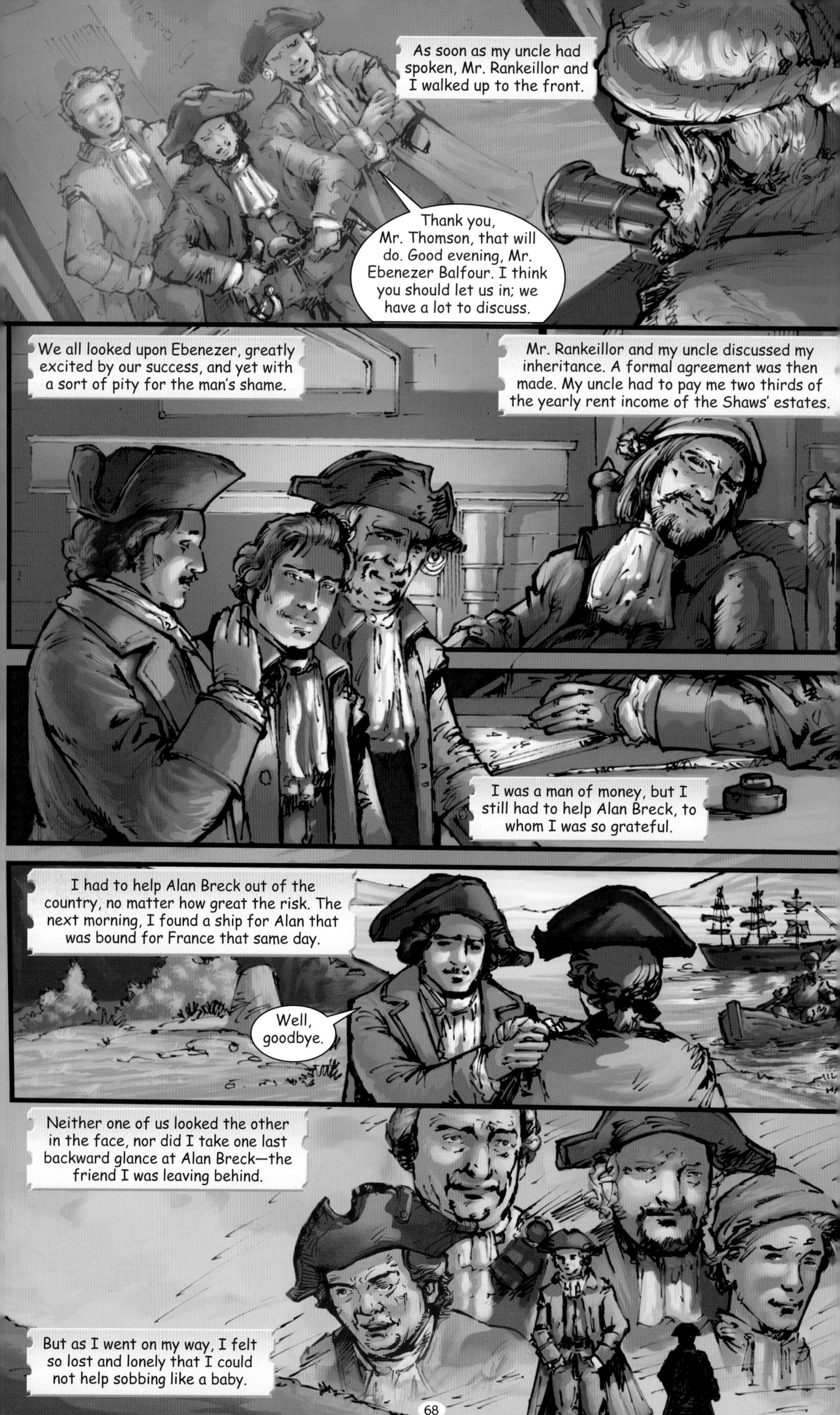

As soon as my uncle had spoken, Mr. Rankeillor and I walked up to the front.
Thank you, Mr. Thomson, that will do. Good evening, Mr. Ebenezer Balfour. I think you should let us in; we have a lot to discuss.
We all looked upon Ebenezer, greatly excited by our success, and yet with a sort of pity for the man's shame.
Mr. Rankeillor and my uncle discussed my inheritance. A formal agreement was then made. My uncle had to pay me two thirds of the yearly rent income of the Shaws' estates.
I was a man of money, but I still had to help Alan Breck, to whom I was so grateful.
I had to help Alan Breck out of the country, no matter how great the risk. The next morning, I found a ship for Alan that was bound for France that same day.
Well, goodbye.
Neither one of us looked the other in the face, nor did I take one last backward glance at Alan Breck—the friend I was leaving behind.
But as I went on my way, I felt so lost and lonely that I could not help sobbing like a baby.

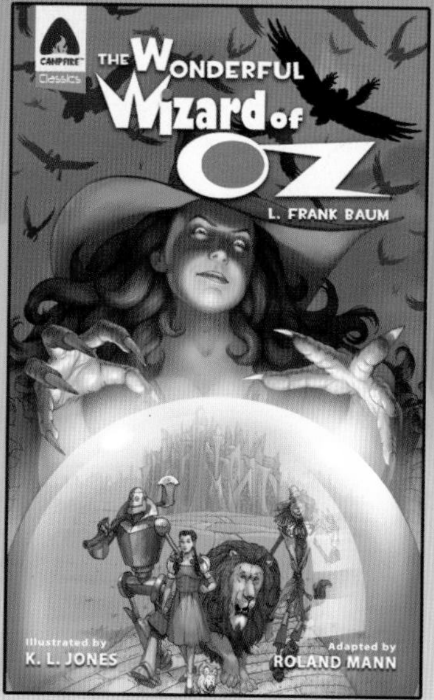
CAMPFIRE Classics
THE WONDERFUL Wizard of OZ
L. FRANK BAUM
Illustrated by
K. L. JONES
Adapted by
ROLAND MANN

L. FRANK BAUM

THE WONDERFUL Wizard of OZ

Adapted by: Roland Mann
Illustrated by: K. L. Jones

A must on everybody's bookshelf, *The Wonderful Wizard of Oz* is a timeless classic that has stirred the imagination of both young and old alike.

A powerful tornado rips through the Kansas prairie catching Dorothy inside her home. Caught inside the vortex, the home floats for hours. When the house finally lands on the ground again, it kills a wicked witch.

Dorothy finds herself in new surroundings and is welcomed by the local inhabitants, the Munchkins, who tell her she is in Oz, surrounded by a great desert that cannot be crossed.

Dorothy's only hope of escape is to see the great Wizard of Oz. On her journey to meet the Wizard, she is joined by some unusual friends who also want favors from the Wizard. But the Wizard will not help Dorothy and her friends unless they do something for him: they must kill the Wicked Witch of the West!

Read on to know more about Dorothy's adventures in this delightful tale that has fascinated children for ages.

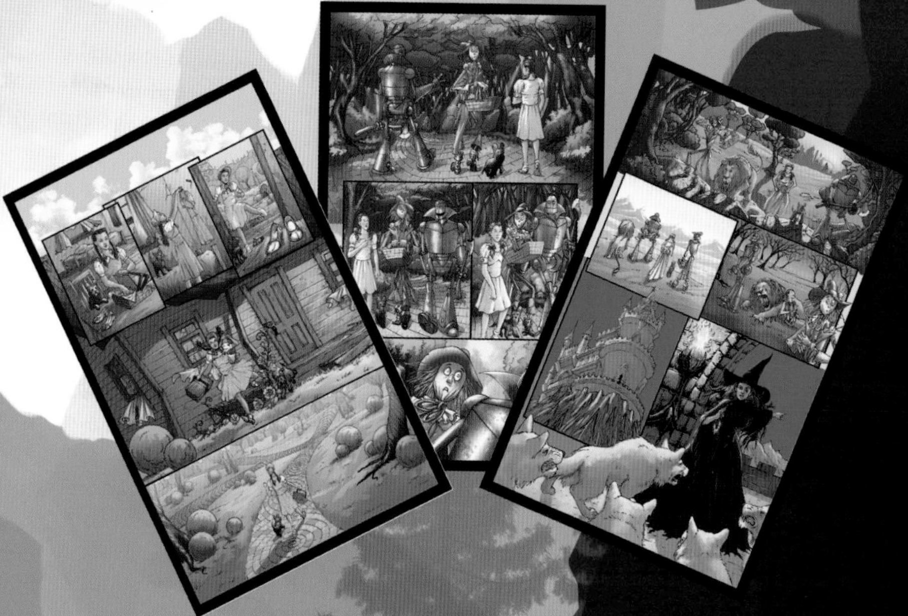

CAMPFIRE™
www.campfire.co.in

Jacobite Risings: The Jacobite Risings were a series of rebellions against the ruling monarchy in England and Scotland. They were attempts to restore the exiled Stuart dynasty to the throne. The Stuart kings were supported by Highlander Scots, who were known as the Jacobites. The Jacobite Risings continued from 1688 until 1746, when the ruling Hanoverian dynasty finally crushed the rebels at the Battle of Culloden. It is the Hanoverian dynasty which continues to rule to this day.

The Highland Charge: The fierce Scots popularized a terrifying attacking strategy called the highland charge during the Jacobite Risings. The highland charge is a very simple and effective way of attacking the enemy. Soldiers charge straight at the enemy and fire their muskets at them from a close distance. Then they hack and slash at the enemy with their claymore swords. A successful highland charge is so terrifying to the enemy that often, the enemy soldiers simply run away at the sight of the charge. Speed and bravery are the keys!